FONGING FOR THE WORLD

FONGING FOR THE WORLD by Jefferson Glassie

Published by:

Peace Evolutions, LLC
Post Office Box 458-51
Glen Echo, MD 20812-0458

Order books from: www.peace-evolutions.com

Printed in the United States.

Book design and cover by Jane Perini

Library of Congress Control Number: 2022914070

ISBN 978-0-9912489-3-3

To my Granddaughters,

Mae and Rosemary,

and to all Granddaughters,

everywhere and for all time.

CONTENTS

9

CHAPTER ONE

THE ANGEL COMES TO ARIA

17

CHAPTER TWO

FONGING BY THE RIVER

29

CHAPTER THREE

MIZZ JOYE IN NEW YORK

49

CHAPTER FOUR

THE DEVI MUSIC ASHRAM IN INDIA

71

CHAPTER FIVE

MUSIC OF THE TREES

97

CHAPTER SIX

THE MUSIC ACT

117

CHAPTER SEVEN

AN ISLAND OUT OF TIME

151

CHAPTER EIGHT

WHAT WAS THAT ABOUT?

159

ONWARD

LOOKING BACK AND
MOVING FORWARD

BY ROY 'FUTUREMAN' WOOTEN

163

BY THE AUTHOR

GRATITUDE

FONGING FOR
THE WORLD

CHAPTER ONE

THE ANGEL COMES TO ARIA

We're going to tell you the story of some humans trying to bring peace to the world through fonging, by tapping into the healing sounds of the universe. So, please, listen up!

* * * * * * *

"I see you, Aria. I see you sleeping there."

Aria wondered in her sleep, "Who is calling my name?"

"Ah, you're awake!"

"Not really," Aria thought. "Is this a dream?" Her eyes were not open, but her ears were awake.

"Ha, come on, child. I know you're listening to me!" This ethereal voice in Aria's brain sure was persistent.

"Who are you?" asked Aria. She opened her mind's eye for a look at the intruder, and saw a golden angel, with actual wings! What was going on?

"I'm here to announce your mission to save the world." The angelic presence seemed confident.

Aria was now fully awake in this dream. "What in heaven's name are you talking about? Uh, are you an angel?"

"Well, I don't just go barging into people's dreams with these golden wings, silver slippers, and sitting on an invisible cloud, unless it has been ordained that I do so." The angel seemed perturbed that Aria didn't realize who or what she was.

"You sure look like an angel, ma'am." Aria decided to be more polite in case this angel had some special powers that could hurt her.

"I'm not going harm you, sweet child."

"She can hear what I'm thinking," thought Aria.

"Of course, I can. Don't you know anything about angels?"

"Sorry," said Aria. "This is just a bit out of the ordinary, if you don't mind me sayin' so." Aria was at least feeling more relaxed in this crazy dream, with her hands clasped behind her head, sitting back, observing. She wasn't scared of this angel anymore and became curious. Save the world?

"Did your grandfather never tell you about me?" The angel asked.

"My grandfather? You mean Bampa?" It wouldn't surprise her if Bampa Erasmus had been talking with an angel.

"Yes, child. I visited him many years ago, a long time ago, and presented to him the ancient gift of fonging. You didn't know that?" The angel seemed incredulous and peered at Aria.

"No, I mean, I don't think so, ah, fonging?" Aria squeezed her eyes and peered up to the virtual night sky, as if searching her memories.

"He wrote a book about it, *Fonging for the Soul*. You don't remember that?" The angel reclined on a gossamer pillow propped up on an invisible cloud.

"Fonging. Fonging? That rings a sliver of a bell." A small bell sounded. "Oh, wait, was that some crazy thing with oven racks? I was pretty young, but I think he told us about it. In fact, I think we did fong, if that's what you call it. That was a long time ago, I don't remember much since then."

The angel sighed. "Well, your grandfather Erasmus really tried, but the fonging overtones didn't quite match with his aural patina as well as we thought they might. I think a lot of people just thought he was crazy."

Her grandfather was a very eccentric man, thought Aria. "Wait, he sometimes called himself the Fongmaster, is that right?"

The angel laughed, "Yes, he did. And that was an appropriate title, for sure." She sighed again. "I'm just not sure people were ready to learn about fonging at the time; or really, to understand the deeper meanings of this ancient art, which enlivens the healing sounds of the universe. Fonging can bring peace to the planet, and even large sentient swaths of the cosmos, by wiping away fear."

Aria thought it sounded like something her grandfather might be involved in.

The angel now became serious. "Aria, it now falls on you to fulfill the intentions of the musical muses. There are still dangers for humankind, and Mother Earth herself. We're calling on you to spread the gifts of fonging around the world, to usher in the new age of *listening*. It's so important. Will you?" The angel pleaded telepathically, you know, like only angels can do.

Aria said, "This is a crazy dream. I'm supposed to save the world through fonging, which I don't even know how to do? Sheesh."

The angel fluttered her wings and some sort of sparkling dust descended all around Aria. "Honey child, we're talking about the healing sounds of the universe. I will teach you the ancient art of fonging. It's pretty cool."

The dusty sprinkles felt really sweet, thought Aria. Sublime. She thought, "Maybe I should listen to this angel."

"Yes, you should listen to me. I can teach you in your dream right now."

This fonging thing was more intriguing than Aria remembered. "OK, fong away, miss angel."

The angel quivered a bit, excitedly, "This is going to be fongtastic!"

Aria's eyes widened, even though closed.

"First, an oven rack."

All of a sudden, Aria was – in her dream – standing and holding a shiny oven rack.

"Perfect," said the angel. "Now take these two shoestrings and tie them around the corners of the narrow end of the rack."

Two white shoelaces appeared in her hands. Aria looked at the strings, then at the rack. Aria always had a can-do attitude. Her grandfather called her the most competent person he ever knew. She would tackle any problem or issue with gusto, doubtless that she would succeed. She also was smart as a whip (however smart a whip might be) and knew she could overcome any challenge. Still, this was perplexing.

"Seriously," she said, "tie these strings to the rack? We're saving the world with an oven rack and shoestrings?"

The angel tilted her head and stared at Aria out of the corners of her eyes.

"Alright, alright," said Aria. She tied a simple knot with each string at the end of the rack. "Now what?"

"Excellent," said the angel. "Now, hold the other end of the strings with your fingers. Wrap the string loosely around each finger, just a wrap or two. Got it?"

Aria followed the instructions and stood there, figuratively speaking, waiting for what to do next.

"Now, lean over slightly from the waist, and gently put your fingers in your ears."

Aria's eyes widened again, and then she recalled a familiar peaceful sensation. "Wow, I do remember this. It's like déjà vu all over again."

"And be sure to have the proper rack dangle; you know, the rack should be even and hanging loosely. Don't let it bang into your tummy." The angel demonstrated, tilting slightly from the waist with an index finger in each ear.

"Right," said Aria. It was coming back to her in an eerie, yet sublimely serene, way. It was almost as if she knew this from another lifetime. Aria leaned from the waist and, with the strings holding the rack up by the fingers, placed her fingers in her ears. She sensed an inner peace, and all other sounds were muffled except her divine within.

"Now, ordinarily," explained the angel, "Your friends or family, or even a stranger, would tap gently on the rack with some kitchen implements, like a serving spoon or wooden ladle, maybe even a screwdriver or a long knife."

"Is this dangerous?" whispered Aria.

"Oh, no," replied the angel. "Fonging is totally safe, and fun for the whole family too! But since we don't have other humans here in the flesh, I've asked some cherub friends to fong with you."

Aria glanced up at the angel, and immediately two small, plump angels appeared; one with a turkey baster and one with a wooden salad fork. She stood straight and took her fingers out of her ears.

"Yikes! What's the deal with the turkey baster!"

"The bulbous end makes a rich harmonious explosive sound when it hits the rack. Very fongtastic; you'll love it," said the angel.

Aria shook her head and thought, "No wonder Bampa didn't talk about fonging much. This is some real crazy stuff. But the angel seems nice."

"Don't you know it, I am nice. Now, Aria, it's time for some healing sounds of the universe."

Aria pursed her lips and sighed. She leaned over a tad from the waist and put her fingers back in her ears. She looked at the cherubs, but the little apparitions just giggled. "OK. Hit it, cherubs."

The two little ones chuckled again, and gently began to tap on the rack with their implements.

Suddenly, the most beautiful sounds she ever heard engulfed Aria's entire body. There was nothing else in her consciousness except some sort of primordial resonance. All her senses were overcome by a vibrational harmony. She floated - immersed - in an ocean of sound.

Then, boom! One of the cherubs swung the turkey baster at the rack and the vibrational cosmos exploded throughout her being!

Aria experienced unbounded joy and unity with everything. Her entire life – past, present, and future - became a colorful song. All her senses blurred together and she felt peace.

The angel and the little cherubs waited for some time with, shall we say, angelic smiles. Angels don't worry about time; it is nothing to them. So, they weren't sure how long Aria stood there with her eyes closed. Neither was Aria.

After a while, she opened her eyes. She felt totally blissed out. She looked at the angel, then the cherubs, and broke out laughing. She let her fingers drift out of her ears, and cackled, chortled, and guffawed.

"Oh, my life. That was the greatest experience I've ever heard. It was like I was in a sea of sound, totally. Thank you so much." She bent down and patted each of the cherubs on the head; they blushed and turned pink.

"Now you understand?"

"Yes, yes I do," replied Aria. Her life had just changed completely, and she had no idea what it meant or what she was going to do next.

"You must go see your grandfather," said the angel. "He will help you. But, let me be clear. You know everything you must do; it will all become obvious. Mainly, just listen. Be open to the vibrations. Listen with your entire being. Sometimes listening means perceiving with your other senses."

Aria sighed and looked at the sky.

"It's time for us to go, dear one. Come along, cherubs."

"Wait," called Aria. "Can I ask a favor, please?"

The angel smiled and said, "Certainly."

"Can you turn my hair purple?"

The angel was surprised, as surprised as angels can be. "That's an unusual request. It's not really in my authorized protocols."

"Oh, come on," implored Aria, now on her knees in the dream, hands folded as if in prayer. She beamed a big smile at the angel. "Pretty please. I've always wanted purple hair since I was a little girl. I just thought maybe you could do that for me. I have a long fonging road in front of me, I think."

The angel tittered and returned the smile. "Oh, why not." She snapped her fingers and whispered, "Abracadabra."

Instantly, Aria's hair turned a sparkling shade of purple. She picked a few strands with her hands and looked at her hair. "Wee, woo! That's so wonderful, thank you angel!"

Aria looked up to hug the angel, but she was gone.

CHAPTER TWO

FONGING BY THE RIVER

"Bampa! ... Bampa 'Rasmus!"

Aria had woken up a while after the angel left, but wasn't sure if she was awake or dreaming, even now. She showered, got dressed, and ate. Then, she had a slew of random things to take care of; she had a feeling she'd be on the move for a while. So, she packed a backpack with clothes, and threw in a blue shaker egg she'd gotten from the Planetary Gigs Society.

It was late afternoon when she finally got to her grandfather's place. He lived at the Namaste Music Ashram near the Potomac River, not too far from Lock 6 of the C&O Canal.

She knocked on the door with one hand, then two. "I know you're in there," she hummed sweetly.

Erasmus had a separate door to his pad, around the side from the main entrance to the Ashram. He opened the door. "Aria, my dear, so nice for you to come by." She came in and gave him a big tight hug.

"Oh, what's all this for? So nice, so nice. My, you have purple hair!" Erasmus said.

"The angel came to see me in my dream last night." She looked him straight in the eye.

"Oh." Erasmus paused. "How is the old gal?" He chuckled, "I'll never forget that visit. Changed my life really, for the good."

"Bamps, fonging is outrageous! She taught me how to fong and I had the most amazing experience! I was enveloped in the most unbelievable sound, like I was suspended in a cosmic soup of vibration. It was crazeballs."

"I can imagine." He exhaled. "Let's sit down."

Aria took off her jacket and cap, putting them on the hat rack by the door. She saw he had a parlor guitar out on a stand, picked it up, and plopped on the couch. Aria always dressed colorfully, various hues of earrings, a long-sleeved cotton top with multi-colored stars, and rainbow striped leggings. She started plucking the strings. "Hmm, open D."

"I've been working on some tunes; I like that little mahogany Martin in open D. Want something to drink?" He asked. Erasmus had been retired for a while now. His thin brown-gray hair was in the semblance of a ponytail, and he had a grayish goatee. Blue Nepali topi, navy flannel shirt, and dark corduroy pants, with a gold cuff in his left ear.

"Naw, I'm good," replied Aria. "So, tell me about your visit with the angel, and what happened after that? I kinda remembered fonging, I mean, a little. But I sure didn't get the whole thing with the primordial sounds."

He sat on an old chair and became serious. "Aria, fonging is really powerful. The angel appeared to me in such a vivid dream and explained I'd been chosen to bring peace to the world through fonging, the healing sounds of the universe, the ancient sound, yada yada. I was down with it, but ... easier said than done."

"The angel said something about the fonging overtones not matching your aural patina." She continued picking the guitar.

Erasmus tilted his head and shrugged his shoulders. "Could be, whatever that means. You know, I wrote a book about fonging. I've got a copy here. It was an instructional text, because no one knew what the hell it was all about; had pictures, too." He reached to the shelf and grabbed a copy, tossing it over to the couch.

"I probably have a thousand left," he continued. "Back in the days before on-demand printing, you know. We had some fun with it, though. We made up the Live, Fong and Prosper shoestrings; the potholder with fonging safety tips; Fong On stickers for your car; and even the Official Fonging Kit, which had a small rack, wooden spoons, all that, you know, for travel and emergency use."

Aria laughed. "Of course, for travel and emergency use. Bampa, who needs to take an oven rack with them for travel and emergency use?"

"Well, my dear, I have a feeling you may."

She sighed.

"People think fonging is totally nuts, Aria. I've fonged with a lot of people. I'm sure more than any other human. You know, June and I took it on the road a couple times. We had people lined up to fong and get free books, and they had such a ball. Inanity is good and worthwhile. I've seen a lot of folks laugh their ears off, so to speak. The whole thing is just ridiculous."

"I know, but Bamps, that sound is incredible. It's deep, it's meaningful."

"I remember one time, I went to a widows and widowers party. Most were not that old; they had faced a lot. After one of them fonged, he said it was the first time since his wife's death that he'd laughed. That was worth it. But it didn't catch on, you know. I suppose I failed, but I don't really believe in failure or mistakes. I believe in doing and learning. I have no regrets. But here you are now; what did the angel say?"

Aria picked a few more chords, then hit the bottom D. "She told me I needed to come see you. Then she said things would become obvious. And she said I had to listen, with my entire being. Just listen." The D faded out.

They sat in silence.

"I have an idea!" Erasmus exclaimed. "I thought up a new fonging method. It'll be perfect to try it with you! So, here's what we'll do. There are some things I'd like to show you in the book. Let's see, the sun will set about 5:30, and we can get something to eat. June and her friend Jennifer are traveling, so we're on our own. Then we'll walk down to the river. It's almost a full moon, and we can look for mergansers. And then, try out this new method. What do you say?"

"I honestly have no idea what to say. Sure, why not."

"This is going to be great!" said Erasmus. He jumped out of his chair and skipped toward the kitchen.

* * * * * *

By the time they had dinner and talked about some important stuff in the book (like fonging etiquette), it was almost 8:00. With the moon nearly full and a steady wind coming down the river from the northwest, they bundled up and headed out the door. It was only a couple blocks to the crossover near Lock 6. They waited till there were no cars, scurried across Canal Road, and a new world opened up.

They walked past the lockhouse, then across the towpath to a foot trail, where they turned south. It was easy to see the path, with the moon shining their way. They heard geese on the river, squawking about something, perhaps an unwanted intruder.

"This is so cool, Bamps," said Aria. "It's the dark sacred night."

Erasmus turned and smiled appreciatively at his grand-daughter. "Yes, my dear, what a wonderful world." He paused, "Now you lead the way."

"But I don't know where I'm going."

"Yes, you do. You always know where you're going."

Aria turned her head and squinted at her grandfather. Without another word, she walked by him and headed down the path. He followed, with his small backpack and walking stick. He used to say, "I can't go for a walk without a stick."

Aria hiked along the soft dirt path, past bare bushes and trees, with the sound of the wind and water all around. She thought, "I don't know where I'm going. Bamps said we're headed to his favorite spot by the river. I'm not sure exactly where that is, particularly in the dark like this, but I know this path is taking me there." She looked ahead and there was no question where to go; she just couldn't see where it ended.

They stopped along the way a couple times, trying to see ducks or geese through the binoculars. Coming to a fork in the path, she went right, toward the river. They went a little further, where there was a good view of the water. She turned and asked in a quiet voice, "This is the way, right, Bamps?"

He nodded. This was the place. There was an old log along the bank, and some big rocks providing a break from the wind. They took off their packs and sat down.

"Brrr," shivered Aria "But wow! This is exhilarating."

"I know. I love the full moon. I think it's called the snow moon in February. And the northwest wind always wakens the spirit. I love it."

Aria shivered. "Spirit's woke for sure, Bamps."

"So, what do you hear?" asked Erasmus.

Aria turned her head toward the moon, looked around the sky. Then, at the trees dancing in the wind, and across the waves on the river. Everything was in motion, moving to some invisible force. She heard geese honking, waves lapping on the rocks, and the pervasive rush of the wind and water. And crackling, swaying branches. "The music of the trees," she said.

Erasmus smiled and whispered, "They say the Aboriginal people don't pray by making pleas to God, but rather they listen. They listen to pray."

Aria closed her eyes. "My soul is full. I hear it calling me. Like an aural tingle. I'm ready to do this, Bampa." She opened her eyes and smiled at him.

He smiled too. "So proud of you, dear, and I really totally love your hair!"

They both laughed.

"You ready to try out that new fonging method?" He opened his pack and pulled out a small toaster oven rack, pre-strung. "For travel and emergency use, and here we are."

Aria shook her head and giggled. "For sure, Bamps."

He also grabbed a wooden spoon and a turkey baster.

"Ok, so you know the basic fonging 'traditional method.' That has one person being fonged. Another one, or even two or more, tapping on the rack. Pretty straightforward, right?"

"Right."

"And then we have the very popular couples fonging. Two people, two racks shared between them, four strings, and any number of tappers you want. It's great because you also hear the racks banging into each other. With me so far?"

"Yes, Bamps. I got this down, jeepers."

"Now, the downside to some of these methods is, if you have just two humans who want to share fonging together, what do you do?" Erasmus looked at her quizzically.

"Hmm. Good question," Aria said. "Doesn't really work with the traditional method; both can't fong at the same time, you know, together." She pondered some more. "And, uh, with the couples method, there'd be no one to tap. Unless, of course, they're just swaying back and forth and hitting the racks together."

"Precisely!" exclaimed Erasmus.

"They wouldn't be able to perceive the nuanced inflections of rhythm and tone they would otherwise experience with some precise tapping." Aria was beginning to feel the groove of this fonging thing.

"You got it! Well said. So, what's the solution?" Erasmus was getting the 'Live, Fong and Prosper' shoestrings untangled from the rack.

"Beats me, Bamps."

"Ah ha! Each person has an index finger with a string in one ear, and taps the rack with the other hand." He seemed proud of himself. "You surrender the full immersion sound experience, with only one ear, but you get to tap yourselves simultaneously, and share the experience. Let's give it a try."

"You've never tried this before?" she asked.

"No, I just thought of it a day or two ago. You'll be the first to experience it with me! You know, I just can't believe it took this long to discover, but hey, important things take time."

They stood up facing one another, took a string from the rack and wrapped it around the index finger on their left hand, and grabbed a utensil with their right hand.

"Wait," said Erasmus. "It's important to set our intention for this fong. We, ... you, have a significant task ahead, perhaps impossible. No matter. If the goal is clear, then mindfully expressing one's intention is the first step to success."

"Wowzers, Bamps. What's the goal?"

"You know, my dear."

"I guess it's to make a difference; to bring some healing to humans and the world, through this crazy – can we call it, spiritual practice? Why not? So many try to create peace in other ways and it hasn't gone so well. Why not try something completely insane? So, that's it, I'm going to listen, like the angel said, and spread the healing sounds however best I can." Aria nodded her head in affirmation.

"Well said, my dear."

"Let's do this," she said.

"OK, ready?" asked Erasmus. They both put their left index fingers in their left ears.

Aria held the turkey baster by the bulbous end, and tapped once, twice, three times on the rack, gently.

"Nice," said Erasmus. He tapped the side, once, loudly with the wooden spoon.

Then she bapped the rack with bulbous end of the turkey baster; boof, boof, boof. "Wow," exclaimed Erasmus.

They proceeded to tap on the rack rhythmically and irrhythmically, varying the touch, where they hit, and soon they both closed their eyes. They swayed a bit in the wind, listening intently to the sounds coming through the rack, the strings, and their fingers. Because they had one ear open, they could also listen to the river and other ambient sounds.

After a few minutes, they paused and opened their eyes. A raft of ducks had gathered on the water near them. A few beautiful white mergansers, painted wood ducks, luminescent mallards, and some larger geese paddled over. A great blue heron presided from a perch on a large rock. Aria saw them, threw her head back, and laughed.

"Bampa, we called the ducks with fonging! How cool is that?"

"My goodness. Those mergansers are normally so skittish, they never allow you to get close. But they're right here looking at us, like they're attending a concert. That was very nice, Aria, I felt that we were literally tapping into the healing sounds."

Aria sat back down on the log. She was still trying to listen to something. She closed her eyes and started gently bobbing her head.

"Some words and music came to me. I'm not sure what it is, or what it means. Let me see if I can get this out." She nodded her head in rhythm, then sang:

I love my path
I trust my goal
I accept myself
I'm on a roll.

"Ah, ha ha, that's it." She smiled and sang it again, grabbed her shaker egg and sang it again.

"Wow, that's fongtastic!" exclaimed Erasmus.

"It just came to me. I heard it when we were fonging, but it wasn't fully formed. Sort of a mantra, right? An affirmation. But it fits; it fits the moment. It's exactly how I feel. I'm ready for this." She smiled confidently at him.

"No doubt, my dear. You're such a badass granddaughter," he said, laughing.

"You got that right." She pointed a finger at him, then became thoughtful again. "Bamps, I had another vision while fonging. I'm not sure what it means. I saw a black and white round mosaic, on the ground. It was near some fields or maybe a park in a city. I had a sense of strawberries. Hmm, wonder what that was about?"

Erasmus sat down. He gazed around at the river, the ducks, and then up to the sky with the full moon. "Was there any writing on the mosaic?"

Aria squinted her mind's eyes, "I just see a letter, it's an I."

The word came to them at the same time. "Imagine."

Erasmus said, "That's the John Lennon memorial; it's

called Strawberry Fields in Central Park, in New York City. There's a mosaic on the ground with the word Imagine in the middle. It's near the apartment where he lived and was shot. So sad."

Aria realized that was it; she had to go to New York, to that memorial.

"I agree," said Erasmus. They both realized he'd heard her thoughts, but didn't say anything about it. They sat quietly and let nature wash over them.

"One thing I have learned from fonging," he continued. "It's about oneness. We're all part of, or maybe emanate from, this ultimate reality of sound, the healing sounds. We're all connected to it and through it. Fonging somehow reflects that deep truth."

"It seems deep, for sure, Bamps." Aria looked around at the river. "In that one session there, I could feel connection, wholeness. Why is it so hard for folks to appreciate all this?" She extended her arms outward.

"I'd say, a perception of separation."

"How do you mean, Bampa?"

"Each of us is unique, different, our own self. We have our own individual fingerprint. But the reality, I believe, is that we're not actually separate; we're part of the whole. Drops in the ocean, stars in the sky. It's not easy to realize. If we perceive that we're not interconnected, we essentially become fugitives from the cosmos."

"That could be a scary place to be," observed Aria.

"That's what fear is. Me versus you, us versus them." Erasmus stood and turned toward the moon. "Another thing I've learned is that – somehow – fonging can heal that perception of being separate. I don't know how, and you don't even have to fong. There's an emanation. A force like a butterfly's wings, which can touch people around the world or start a hurricane across the ocean."

"Hmm. I'm diggin' it. A little of the healing sounds goes a long way."

"Yes, and I believe fonging can resolve particular areas of concern and insecurity. Keep that in mind."

"I will, I will." Aria wondered what that would mean for her.

With that, they gathered up their fonging paraphernalia, said good-bye to their avian audience, and walked the path back to the Music Ashram. Aria slept on a couch and hung around the next day to spend some more time with her grandfather. She jammed a little with him and a couple other musicians. She was mainly a singer, but played piano and guitar, too. They watched some music videos and there was an open mic on the Namastage.

Erasmus gave her a couple small racks and some other fonging paraphernalia for her trip. She said goodbye and went to bed early to get on the road to New York. She was eager to get on with this adventure.

CHAPTER THREE

MIZZ JOYE IN NEW YORK

The maglev train to New York flew down the rails. Aria bought a ticket on her phone and got a lyft to the station early. She wanted to stay and hang out with her grandfather, but also felt anxious to get going. She said she would holog him later.

She pulled the tray down and set up her computer to do some course work. She was getting her graduate degree in matriarchal studies, and had majored in music and history in college. So many things had changed since the pandemic. Graduate courses could be taken anywhere, and the curriculum had become much advanced, more segmented, and curiously less time consuming. It seemed many things had become more efficient after the pandemic.

Some called it the Great Realization. People learned what they valued and eliminated a lot of unnecessary tasks and materialistic stuff. Many got new jobs or started different careers. There was more emphasis on helping others. The social safety net had been strengthened. Health care was much more affordable, though not free for all. Some funding had been moved from the military and police to social programs. There was more sense of community, in the country and around the world.

Nonetheless, there were ongoing problems. Greed and excess continued in the financial markets. Some religions had become more reactionary. Discrimination and racism unfortunately were not cured, yet. Sexual assaults were common enough that women still didn't feel safe taking walks in many places. Humans continued to degrade the planet. And a faction of the populace continued to worship fascistic politicians who hadn't given up on the idea of maintaining the upper white caste.

These were some of the issues that Aria assumed the angel wanted her to tackle with fonging. She wasn't sure how to do that other than take it one step at a time.

She arrived in New York and decided to walk from Penn Station to Central Park. Even though it was a chilly February day, the sun was out. She walked up 7th Avenue and took her time. It was fun looking in store windows and watching people. She thought some of the stores looked like only rich people could shop there, and outside on the streets there were people begging for money.

Aria wondered what she was going to do when she got to Strawberry Fields. She had no specific plans, and no place to stay. All she really knew to do was keep her ears open.

She continued her trek, and entered Central Park by the south entrance, at 59th and 7th. She meandered through the Park, checking the kiosk maps to make sure she was headed in the right direction. Strawberry Fields was on the west side, near The Dakota hotel where John Lennon, and many other celebrities, had lived.

She finally arrived. It was a very peaceful spot, designated a quiet zone. The sign said no musical instruments were allowed; that seemed odd. Maybe it was to keep the place from being a perpetual jam session. It was near a small body of water called the Lake. Quite a few people were milling around.

She walked over and stood at the Imagine mosaic. Just like she had seen in her vision, it was a black and white round tile mosaic, with the word Imagine in the center. It was very powerful; John Lennon touched so many people. The music created by the Beatles had literally changed the world. She felt humbled, and grateful.

Then, Aria thought she heard a guitar. Where was that coming from? She looked around and finally saw a guitar player by the Lake. She went over to check it out.

As she got closer, she could hear an acoustic guitar and singing. The musician was an old black woman, with a poof of white hair on her head. She was wearing coverall jeans, with a multicolored kente cloth jacket and white scarf, and red high-top sneakers. Aria got close, stood silently for a while, and listened.

The woman finished her song with a flourish and bowed to the lake. Aria clapped. The woman turned around and said, "I was hoping you were going to clap. I think it's a good song."

"I love it," said Aria. "Let's take money off the altar, for sure."

"I wrote it for John. You know there's that line in his song, 'Imagine no possessions.' I keep thinking about that. What if we did have an entirely different sort of economic system? What would that look like?"

Aria replied, "I hear you. Why is everything about money? We're sort of forced to believe that humans are takers and just want more and more; it's like a social construct. I'm kinda sick of it all frankly. I think if everyone was just able to do their passion and help support their community, it would all work out."

"That's powerful medicine right there. We're on the same page. I'm gonna go over and sing my song in the circle."

"Great idea, but it says no musical instruments on the sign," Aria pointed out.

"Well, that's just the craziest thing I ever heard; no playing music at the John Lennon memorial? I don't think he'll mind." She pulled the guitar off her shoulder. "So, what's your name, pretty girl? That purple hair is boss."

"My name's Aria, nice to meet you. What's yours?"

"My name is Joye, same as my religion. Howdy doo." Joye had a cascade of silver earrings in both ears.

"That sounds like my kinda religion. Mind if I call you Mizz Joye?" said Aria.

"Sure, that would be fine," replied Joye.

"And can I shake along with your song?" Aria had set her pack down and pulled out the blue shaker egg, holding it up to show Joye.

"That's what I'm talking about; c'mon over with me. Do you sing? Here are the words. They can toss us both in jail," Joye laughed and handed her the lyrics on a folded sheet of paper.

Aria looked at the words and nodded her head. "I think I got it, Mizz Joye."

"Let's cut it up, Aria." They walked over to the mosaic,
put their packs down, and stood in the center of the mosaic.

"Ladies and gentlemen," called out Joye. "My friend
and I are gonna perform a song I wrote for John, or at least
inspired by his song, Imagine. We hope you'll enjoy it. 1 -2 -3
..." Joye started playing and Aria shook her shaker in time.

Money is like a river
Just sayin', it needs to flow.
If it gets hung up in a bank vault somewhere,
The kids downstream cannot grow.

It's just the same, with your blood
It needs to get to those extremities.
If it gets all clogged up in your heart,
It'll bring you right down to your knees.

So, let's take money off the altar
Let's focus on what's good and right.
We can all live and be together
And sing our song into the night.

It seems to be the same in society
Everybody needs a little dough.
But if there's too many of those friggin' billionaires
There's not enough coin to show.

So, let's take money off the altar
Focus on what's good and right.
We can all live and be together
And sing our song into the night,
And sing our song into the night.

The crowd clapped and cheered. Aria and Joye bowed together and hugged.

"That was fun, Aria. Let's sit over here and chat." She led them to a vacant part of the bench toward the Lake.

Aria took a swig of water from her bottle and relaxed on the bench. "That seemed like it was meant to happen. Why did you come here today, Mizz Joye?"

Joye said, "I don't know. I've been working on that song, finished it a few days ago. But I woke up this morning, just live right over there in Brooklyn, and I got a vision of this place and had to come."

"Me, too," said Aria. She was trying to decide how much to tell Joye, and just thought the truth was best. "Actually, an angel came to me in a dream and told me I'm supposed to bring peace to the world through – don't think I'm crazy – this thing called fonging. I was hanging out with my grandfather Erasmus the night before last on the banks of the Potomac River and I got the vision. The Imagine mosaic. I just had to come." Aria shrugged her shoulders and smiled sheepishly at Joye.

Joye stared at Aria. Then, she put her hand to her mouth and shook her head. "Oh, my lord. Fonging. Erasmus."

Aria's eyes got wide. "You know about fonging? You know my grandfather, Mizz Joye?"

After a moment, they broke out laughing, so loudly some folks looked over.

"Let me tell you. Not only do I know fonging and your grandfather, lordy me, but my picture is on the front of that crazy thing he was trying to sell, what was it, the Fonging Kit. No lie. My picture's in the book a few times, too."

"In *Fonging for the Soul*? No way!" Aria grabbed the book out of her pack and flipped through the pictures. "Oh my god, this is you, right here! Wowzers! Mizz Joye!" They both were giggling.

"I can't believe this," said Joye. "But, you know, I can. There was always something mystical about this fonging stuff. So, the angel came for you. I guess the old Fongmaster needed some help."

"It was amazing, Mizz Joye. The angel shows up in my dream, tells me I have to save the world by bringing the healing sounds of the universe through fonging. She tells me to listen, just listen. So, I have a vision, I come up here, I hear you, and you know all about fonging and my grandfather. Yikes."

"There are no coincidences, my child. I'm sure I'm supposed to help you now. But how?'

"I have no idea what we're gonna do, Mizz Joye."

"Well, one step at a time. I'm hungry. Let's go over toward The Dakota, there's a little diner near there. We can talk."

"Sounds like a plan, Mizz Joye." They gathered up their things and walked out of the park.

They got a table in the window and waited to order. "You know, Aria, I've been fighting for peace and justice my whole life. Felt like that little child with his finger in the dike. Grew up in apartheid in Fredericksburg, Virginia. For so long, I wanted to be white. Straightened my hair, all that. But you know what happened? I learned to love myself. I became liberated by the blues."

"I love blues music. So emotional; so true. Were you in a band?

"Indeed, I was. For almost 30 years. We were the Uppity Blues Women. Traveled all over the world. Had a fan base with mainly a lot of middle aged and older women. I've written some kick-ass songs in my life, Aria." She laughed. "I also have many sheroes; Nina Simone, Big Mama Thornton, Alberta Hunter. Strong women, yea. They helped me along the way. And not easy for a gay black woman, too."

"That's so inspiring," said Aria.

"Been trying to right so many wrongs. Racial injustice. Economic hardships. Sexual discrimination and harassment. So many people suffering. I do think it's been heading in the right direction after that pandemic we had, but the rich just keep getting richer."

"Hey, look at that limo out there on the street. I've never seen one so big. What's that license plate say?" Aria was trying to read it. "It says GOLIATH."

"You mean, GOLIATH Enterprises? That Alexander Bozos is one of the richest men on the planet. I'd like to give him a piece of my mind. Is he there?" Joye was craning her neck to see.

"Is he the guy with the big G on his cap? He looks like he's coming in here!"

"My, my, my," said Joye. "I'm going to call him out, you know ..."

Aria interrupted. "No, I have an idea. Let's see if we can get him to fong."

"What, girlfriend? I think that angel sprinkled too much fairy dust on you or something."

"Really, Mizz Joye. We'll fong with him. This is our chance to inject some healing sounds right into his soul. C'mon, let's try," said Aria. She stood up just as Alexander Bozos entered the diner.

"Do you have my mushroom soup ready?" Bozos called out loudly so everyone would hear. The waiter nodded and scurried to the kitchen.

Aria walked over to him. "Mr. Bozos, I presume? I saw your car out there, with the license plates. Do you think we could share some healing sounds with you?"

Bozos was surprised. He put an arm around Aria and said, "Nice purple hair, chickie."

"So, you like mushroom soup, huh?"

"I have it every day."

"Could me and my friend Mizz Joye have some soup with you? And then we could demonstrate the healing sounds, too. They're really powerful vibrations. There's this technique we use called fonging."

Joye couldn't believe what was happening, but she decided to roll with it. "I'd really like to help you hear the healing sounds, Mr. Bozos."

Bozos was somewhat taken aback. No one had ever offered to fong with him before. He didn't know what it was, but it sounded intriguing.

"Maybe you could get some extra soup for us, and we'll come up to your place and fong a little. What do you say?"

asked Aria. She was looking right into his eyes.

Bozos called to the waiter, "Two more soups to go."

Soon, Aria and Joye were riding in the back seat of the GOLIATH Enterprises limo with Alexander Bozos, heading to his luxury condo. Bozos was not a tall man, and his bald head shined when he took off his cap. The limo was very fancy, and he offered them a drink from the bar.

"No, thanks," said Aria, "But I'm looking forward to some soup. It must be really good."

"Oh, yea," said Bozos. "So, what are these sounds about? Do you play this guitar you have here?"

"Actually, no, not to fong. But you're going to love it, Mr. B," replied Aria. "Fonging involves some kitchen implements, and an oven rack. You have an oven, right?"

"Of course, I have one of the best ovens money can buy," said Bozos.

"I'm sure you do," said Joye.

Bozos announced, "Here we are ladies. Short ride. Wait'll you see the view of Central Park from my top floor condominium." He got out of the car and held the door open for them.

They walked up to the glass entryway, which said: BIG BOZOS BUILDING in large gold letters.

"Hey, is this the old Trump Tower?" asked Joye, staring up almost sixty floors.

Bozos laughed, "He didn't need it in jail, so I bought it at bankruptcy to spite him."

"Lordy, we should've ordered more than just mushroom soup," said Joye as they entered.

They rode up the elevator to the top floor and got out. Bozos opened the door, and they entered a ginormous condo.

Aria and Joye were drawn over to the glass doors and balcony overlooking Central Park.

"Wow, look at this! What a view. Mr. B, this is totally dope," exclaimed Aria.

"Nice situation, man," said Joye.

Bozos glowed in the praise. "I deserve this, with all I have done to create and run our company. Just think of all the good it does for people all over the world, improving their daily lives. They only have to think of ordering something and it arrives pronto!"

Joye held her tongue, barely. Aria walked over to Bozos. "So, should we fong before soup?"

Bozos smiled and rubbed his hands together. "We can always heat up the soup later."

"OK, Mr. B, but we're gonna need a few things to fong. Mizz Joye, let's see if he has some nice racks in the kitchen. I have travel racks, but big racks sound best. We need some kitchen utensils. Hopefully, there's a turkey baster in there."

Bozos seemed excited and terrified at the same time. "Turkey baster?"

Aria said, "Everyone I have ever fonged loves the turkey basters."

Bozos was speechless.

Then Aria said, "And we're going to need some shoe-strings. Let's see your shoes." With that, she led him the couch, pushed him down, kneeled on the floor, and grabbed his feet. "Look at these pointy shoes. The shoestrings are kinda pathetic. What are we gonna do?"

Bozos said, "Shoestrings?"

"Yea, to tie onto the racks," explained Joye.

Aria went into the kitchen with Joye and they rummaged around.

"Here's a nice clean rack, and a drawer with some utensils. Take your pick," said Joye.

"Man, what a sweet wooden salad fork, and this metal ladle is sweet. Score, spatula. Yay, a turkey baster; the bulb is even shaped like a turkey. So cool!" She glanced at Joye's shoes. "Red Chuck Taylor's! Can we use those strings, Mizz Joye?"

"Well, I guess I can lend them to the cause," said Joye.

They returned to Bozos with the rack and utensils, and Joye sat down next to Bozos and started taking the strings out of her shoes. "You are gonna love this. You will never be the same."

Bozos hadn't moved.

"Alright, Mr. B. Let's do this. Stand up," commanded Aria.

Joye tied her shoestrings at the corners of the narrow side of the rack. "Now we're talking."

Aria took control. "Stand up, stand up."

Bozos stood up.

"Now, hold this rack up by the strings, and wrap the strings lightly around the index finger of each hand. Not too tight; don't want to cut off the circulation. That's it."

Bozos was overwhelmed by their energy. He had surrendered.

"Alright," said Aria. "Lean over slightly from the waist, so the rack doesn't bang on your stomach. Now, put your fingers in your ears."

He looked at her in bewilderment. "What?"

"Put an index finger in each ear."

"You heard what the lady said," urged Joye.

"Listen, you're going to love this and thank us sooner than you can imagine," said Aria.

Bozos leaned over, put his fingers in his ears and stood there, silently. Aria and Joye both knelt in front of him. They looked at one another, and closed their eyes momentarily while offering the intention of bringing the healing sounds to this materialistic man.

Aria lightly touched the rack with the big wooden fork. Once, twice, three times. Joye hit the side of the rack more loudly with the ladle. They waited a moment to let the sounds penetrate his consciousness. They could tell he felt it. His eyes were closed. Then, they began to play a slightly off-rhythm song of sorts. They drew the utensils across the tines, quickly, then slowly.

After a few minutes of this, Aria started using the tip end of the turkey baster and Joye tapped with a metal spatula, one end then the other. Bozos began to sway.

Finally, Aria flipped the baster around and bapped the rack with the bulbous end. Boof, boof, boof. The rack recoiled and she let it swing, then bopped it sharply again. BOOF! Then, they stopped and let the silence soothe him.

Bozos was drooling a little, with his eyes still closed. They thought he might tip over, but he stayed standing. For quite some time.

Joye grew concerned and whispered, "Is he breathing? We didn't kill him, did we?"

"He's breathing," replied Aria.

"Whew, I didn't want them to say we assassinated him," said Joye.

Aria closed her eyes and listened. She thanked him for receiving this experience. She felt compassion for him. She felt love for him.

Bozos took a long breath. He shook his head gently. "Oh my God." He stood, opened his eyes, then closed them again.

"Why don't you sit right here," said Joye, leading him to the couch. He sat down, still disoriented. She got him a glass of water, which he took with both hands, and swallowed deeply.

He opened his eyes wide, shook his head, and looked at each of them. "That was unbelievable, ladies. What in the world? I mean, I thought ... fonging, I didn't know, uh." He paused. "I feel like I've been reborn. Like I see with new eyes; hear with new ears."

"It's some pretty powerful energy, the healing sounds of the universe, huh?" asked Aria.

"Is that really what that was? I felt I was in a place without time, with sound all around. I was immersed in vibration. You know, I did feel healed, of what I don't know."

"Mr. Bozo," said Joye, "I mean, Bozos. I believed you may have been healed of greed; of an insatiable desire for money. Greed is a powerful insecurity."

Bozos reflected on that. "My whole life, I wanted to achieve financial success. We have an awesome company. We help people out a lot, everyday."

"But you have more money than Fort Knox, don't pay tax, and still don't even pay your workers what they deserve. How much money do you need? I can tell you, there are billions of people who need money more than you. What does it help them for you to go to space? People don't have enough to get by, even to feed their families, all over the world."

Joye stood up, pacing around the room, and continued. "I grew up in poverty, yes I did. All the black folks I knew worked hard, but everything was stacked against them. Same for the white folks living out in the country. This economic system treats so many people just like dirt, while the rich people siphon off bank loads of money. Poverty just annihilates the future. When you got nothing, you got nothing to lose. What little money you get, why not spend it on booze and cigarettes? There is some staggering fear in poverty and being kept down for so long, it's just so debilitating. Don't you care about other people? Have you no empathy, sir?"

Bozos hung his head.

Aria chimed in. "Greed's the same as poverty, just the opposite. We see billionaires act like they're terrified not to get richer. It seems to me it's an insane paranoia when someone thinks there's never enough money for them."

Bozos agreed, "I always wanted more. You know, go to the moon and stars!" He paused. "But I don't have that desire anymore. It's just gone. All of a sudden, gone. I just feel this wholeness. Fullness. From the fonging. I'm going to change."

Aria cheered, "Woo Hoo! That's awesome Mr. B. So exciting! You can do so much."

"What are you gonna do?" asked Joye.

He thought. Then raised his fist. "We're going to pay everyone in our company at least $50 an hour!"

Joye clapped. "But you know that's what it should be, at least, if wages had just kept up with inflation all these years!"

Bozos continued, "And GOLIATH will pay full health care and benefits, child care, maternal and paternal time off, six months, why not!" He got up and pranced around the room with Joye. "And we should help fund retirement, too. Think of all the good we can do. People will really like me! What do you think, Mizz Joye?"

"Yea, and it will be the right thing to do. People shouldn't have to worry so much about money just to get by, especially in such a wealthy country as ours. The pandemic showed us who the real essential workers are, but also how they can slip through the safety net. Other companies will see what GOLI-ATH is doing and will change, too. You personally can have a huge impact on the country, and on the world."

"Oh, ladies. I am so glad to have met you. I loved the fonging. Thank you."

"This is so swell, Mr. Bozos. Now, a couple of things," said Joye. "Can I get my shoestrings back please. And can we have some of that mushroom soup? I'm a hungry woman!"

"Of course, of course. Let's go in the kitchen and heat it up." Bozos and Joye literally danced into the kitchen.

Aria looked out the window at Central Park. She couldn't believe what had happened to her in the short time since the angel visited. She didn't know what was next, but she'd accept whatever it was going to be.

Her gaze fell on a golden statue on a side table next to the wall. Was it really gold? A saint or a god, it seemed. With thick hair, a crescent moon by his head, and what looked like a snake around his neck. He held a trident, and there was a third eye in the middle of his forehead. She couldn't look away from it.

Then, she noticed some music playing. Where was that coming from? She looked around, but it seemed to be only in her mind. Was that a sitar?

Joye and Bozos returned with the soup. "Here you go Aria, it smells delish," said Joye.

"Mr. B. What is that statue? Is that Shiva?" asked Aria.

"Why yes, it is. I was so taken by it at an art show. They said he's the destroyer in Hinduism or something. That really appealed to me." He placed the soup on the coffee table, sat on the couch, and started slurping. "Hmm, so good."

"Damn right," agreed Joye.

"But Mr. B, Shiva is also considered the god who creates and protects the universe. He's very powerful," said Aria.

"I guess that's why I liked him, too," laughed Bozos.

"Does anyone else hear Indian music?" asked Aria.

Joye tilted her head, "Um, no."

Just then, Aria's device vibrated. She grabbed it out of her back pocket and looked at the screen. "My grandfather's calling. I'm going to put him on holog; I'm sure you have 8-X here, right, Mr. B?"

"Of course, I do." He continued slurping.

Aria set the device on the table, and said, "Accept."

In a few moments, a three-dimensional image of Erasmus was standing on the table, about two feet high.

"Ah, Aria, I had to check on you. I was hearing some sitar music in my head and thought I should holog. How are you?" Erasmus had a smile on his face as he looked at his granddaughter.

"Holy smokes, Bamps, I was hearing the same thing. Believe it or not, I ran into an old friend of yours at Strawberry

Fields. You remember Mizz Joye, right here."

Erasmus looked around. "Well, well, Joye, Joye. So amazing to see you. Not hard to believe Aria ran into you."

"You're looking fine, old friend. You have a wonderful granddaughter."

"Also, you won't believe this, Bamps, we just finished fonging with Alexander Bozos up here in his posh condo overlooking Central Park. He had a great experience and he seems to be a new man. Mr. Bozos, this is my grandfather; he's the Fongmaster."

"Nice to meet you, Fongmaster. I'm impressed," said Bozos. "That fonging is incredible stuff. These are some fine young ladies, too."

"So glad you were able to experience that, Mr. Bozos. Sometimes we can change dramatically when we least expect it. Honestly, fonging often does that."

"Well," said Bozos. "More people should experience it."

Erasmus said, "I believe it can ameliorate fears in particular areas. Like insecurities around money. The system we have is based on fear and scarcity, and the idea that people are just greedy."

"Aren't they?" asked Bozos

"No, not at all, Mr. Bozos," replied Erasmus. "Humans are creators and contributors, if we just let them not have to worry so much about money all the time. It's debilitating."

"That's what I've been telling him," added Joye. "I think he's beginning to get it."

Aria thought she'd change the subject. "My grandfather lives in a music ashram, Mr. B. It's pretty cool."

"What's a music ashram, Fongmaster?" asked Bozos.

"Well, it's an intentional community, any size, where people live and share resources, but the focus is on music and the arts. We play and learn together. Teach classes. It saves everyone money, there are always plenty of people to help out with things, and we love music."

"Hmm," said Bozos. "You know, the real estate market has been transformed since the pandemic. Many offices have been turned into housing units. The Tower has a lot of vacant units."

"You should turn it into a music ashram, Mr. B," said Aria.

"What an excellent idea, Aria," said Bozos. "I'll get to that right after I finish my soup."

"Bamps, check out that statue of Shiva over there in Mr. B's condo. It called out to me somehow."

Erasmus turned to look at the statue. He closed his eyes.

"What is it, Bamps?"

"I think we have to go to Rishikesh, to the Devi Music Ashram. You, me, and Mizz Joye. I'll work out the logistics and get back to you." With that, his image disappeared.

CHAPTER FOUR

THE DEVI MUSIC ASHRAM IN INDIA

Aria went with Joye to her place to pack, then they took the train to D.C. and stayed at the Namaste Music Ashram overnight. It was quite a homecoming for Joye and Erasmus, who hadn't seen one another for years. They spent some time getting their logistics together for the trip. Erasmus managed to get tickets and visas online quickly, so they could leave the next day. They were able to play some music together that night, too.

They left from Dulles airport the next evening and arrived in Delhi, India in the morning. Erasmus had called his friend Raj at the Devi Music Ashram, who happened to be in Delhi and picked them up at the airport.

"Namaste, Raj, so good to see you again," said Erasmus, bending forward with his hands folded.

"Yes, Erasmus. Namaste. It is wonderful to see you too," said Raj. He presented them with garlands of white and yellow marigold flowers.

Erasmus introduced them all around. Then, they packed their bags and instruments into Raj's car. Raj wore a saffron cotton shirt and a multicolored topi.

"There's a lot of smog or something in the air," said Joye.

Erasmus said, "Believe it or not, it's better now than when I was here years ago. We were wearing facemasks then for the pollution, before the pandemic."

"Yes, indeed, you are right," added Raj. "The air became much more clear during the pandemic when we were on lock-down for so long. You can put a facemask or a bandana or something like that over your mouth and nose if you would like. In the car, it should not be so bad."

The four of them piled into the car. Raj drove, with the steering wheel on the right side. They drive on the left like the British, a remnant of colonization.

Immediately, Aria and Joye realized they weren't in the United States anymore. Cars and motorbikes and busses drove in every available space, honking, starting, stopping. Raj narrowly avoided an ox cart loaded with sugar cane. They jostled around in their seats and held on to the handles. Raj drove skillfully and soon they were outside of the main city district.

"Maybe I should ask," said Aria, "Where exactly are we going?"

Raj replied, "Rishikesh is about an eight-hour drive north-west toward the Himalayas. That is where the Devi Music Ashram is located, on the Ganga River. You will meet Neeru there. We are going to stop for the night in Haridwar on the way. We will go to the aarti and puja ceremony tonight. I think you will like it."

Joye was looking out the window, bracing herself as the car zipped in and out of traffic. "Look at all the cows. Just walking around everywhere. Cars and trucks, and people walking around, in and out of the street. No sidewalks, just hard dirt. And trash everywhere. This is amazing."

Just then a car came within inches on the left, honked its horn, careened around a skinny brown cow, and accelerated ahead. Raj remained calm, and carried on.

"You know what I'm noticing," said Aria. "It seems chaotic, but actually the traffic flows very efficiently. And the drivers aren't honking their horns because they're angry. They're telling other vehicles where they are; they're signaling so other drivers can hear them and avoid crashing into them. This whole traffic situation seems very musical to me."

"Indeed, you are right, Aria," said Raj. "It is a little herky and jerky, but since there are so many people, this is how we avoid accidents. One must remain alert and keep eyes and ears open."

"So interesting," said Aria, "It's like a big traffic concert. Quite an efficient flow. I'm digging it. Also, Raj, the way you speak is very musical, too. I love listening to you."

"Thank you, Aria. It is a pleasure that you all are here."

They rode for several hours, taking a couple of breaks, and the countryside became more rural. Erasmus advised when they stopped that they only eat cooked or pre-packaged food, and only drink water that had been boiled, or out of bottles with the seal intact. One can become quite sick in India eating the wrong food or drinking the water. He said not even to brush your teeth with tap water, only bottled water.

They arrived in Haridwar late afternoon and found a nice

hotel. After they settled in, Raj had them get back in the car and they drove to the site of the aarti along the Ganga River. They parked and got out of the car into a sea of humanity. Many of the native Indians stared at them. Merchants called out to buy some of their wares. A man with no legs dressed in dirty white clothes held his hand out begging. Would he be one of the so-called untouchables? A few poor children ran up begging for money.

Raj said, "You must ignore them for now." He told the children to leave the foreigners alone.

"This is so sad on many levels," said Aria.

"Yes, an amazing and beautiful land of many contrasts," agreed Erasmus.

Raj called out for their attention. "We will stop and buy you all some clothes. You will feel more comfortable, you know, not standing out. And you will be less of a target for beggars and those wanting your money. We can go into a shop I know down this alley here. They have some nice clothing."

Erasmus was wearing an Indian style white block collar shirt and a vest, but he bought a white silk kurta, another vest, and a new topi. The more interesting shopping involved the women. The shop keeper asked them to sit down and offered them tea and some snack food. Raj nodded that they could eat the cookies. The shop keeper looked at Aria and Joye and determined what clothes would be best for them.

As a young, unmarried woman, he brought Aria a salwar suit in blue, yellow, and purple. He also brought some silver bangles.

"Hey, I'm liking this, Bamps. Beautiful clothes and some

boss jewels and stuff."

Joye was a mother, older, and not now married, so the shop keeper brought her a red sari to try on, with glass bangles. "I love my coveralls, but this is going to be fun. Feel this silk. Kinda exotic, don't you think?"

Erasmus complimented them. "Yes, exquisite."

"Very lovely," Raj agreed.

The shop keeper brought them several variations and soon they settled on a couple to buy. Very inexpensive compared to the U.S.

Raj said, "Now we can go get a seat for the ceremony. Please follow me."

They stuck behind Raj as he crossed a bridge and walked over to the main steps where the ceremony was taking place. He found seats for them as the program began. There were many people in attendance from all walks of life. This program was conducted every evening, and there was an air of excitement in the crowd.

The puja ceremony started with several pujari in orange attire singing chants from steps that led right into the river. Many people stood on the steps with their feet in the water. Soon, the priests began to pour milk into the river while they prayed. The singing continued.

Then, they started banging on bells, and lit oil fires that they held aloft in brass lamps, moving them in circles. Soon more fires were lit, music began to play, then more singing. This seemed like the highlight. Other people began placing lotus leaves with candles, incense, and flowers on the water, which flowed down the river.

Aria was mesmerized. "So amazing; so moving."

"I've never seen anything like this," said Joye. "It's so spiritual."

"Yes, this is very special ceremony, aarti," said Raj. "It is a part of the puja, at the end of the prayers. The word aarti comes from 'aa,' which means completeness, and 'rati,' which means love. So, we offer full love to the gods. The flame is offered to them. One can offer to whichever god or goddess one likes to."

"There are many gods in Hinduism, yes?" asked Joye.

"Indeed, there are many," replied Raj. "Some people say there are 33 gods, but some say there are 330 million gods. There can be gods for anything, and each person has their own gods. I would say that the gods represent different forces and elements; there are stories to explain some basic principles. Like in the Bhagavad Gita, for example."

Erasmus added, "I've learned to view the stories of the Christian religion and the Bible the same way. They're essentially myths that can teach basic truths. We can rise again from troubles in our life, that sort of thing."

When it was over, they followed Raj back to the car. On the walk back along the Ganga, Joye was cornered by a woman who encouraged her to buy a lotus flower with the candle and incense, so she could place it in the river. Joye did as suggested and watched the flaming flower boat go down the Ganga. The woman also gave her cup after cup of milk for Joye to pour into the river. And then, of course, she wanted money. But it was only 50 rupees, which was under a dollar.

"Everyone sure does want your money; lucky thing, it's not too much for us," said Joye. She gave the woman money and bowed to her with hands folded. "Namaste."

The next morning, they packed into the car again and drove off to Rishikesh. Along the way, they saw many temples and large statues of Shiva, and they continued their conversation about religion.

"Most of the people in India are Hindu, I think 80 percent," said Raj. "Then, some Muslim, and smaller percentages of the other major religions. Christianity, Sikhism, Buddhism, Jainism, Zoroastrianism, Judaism, and Baha'i Faith are also practiced in India. I would say that these religions represent an opportunity to have conversations about life and spirituality, rather than dogma."

"Since there are 1.3 billion people in India, even a small percentage in one religion could be a lot folks!" said Erasmus. "In the 1940's when Gandhi was alive and leading protests for Indian independence, there were only about 350 million people, so they added a billion people since that time."

"His example of nonviolence to lead the Indian people out of control of the British was very acclaimed," said Raj.

"Martin Luther King was also influenced by Gandhi's non-violent approach," added Joye.

Aria said, "There is so much complexity in India."

Soon, they arrived at the Devi Music Ashram outside Rishikesh. It was quite a large compound, about six acres. It had been the ashram of Maharishi Mahesh Yogi for Transcendental Meditation, where the Beatles had visited in 1968. That was quite a synergistic moment in spiritual and musical time. Neeru turned it into a Music Ashram after the pandemic.

A large open music amphitheater was in the center, with a kitchen and dining hall, a garden, a residence building with

40 sleeping rooms, and many music classrooms that had been meditation chambers. Most interesting were the eighty-four individual river stone abodes, each with a sleeping room, kitchenette, toilet, and a meditation room on the top.

"Wow, look at this place," exclaimed Aria. There were people dressed in Indian clothing walking around, some sitting and playing guitars, sitars, and other instruments. "I could live here for a while."

"Pretty amazing, that's for sure," added Joye.

Raj showed them to their rooms and said they could relax, wander around, and check everything out until dinner time. "Please feel free to do as you like. We will see Neeru at dinner."

* * * * * * *

They met in front of the dining hall before dinner. Neeru was sitting in a red velvet chair in the lobby area. She was an elegant woman and wore a blue sari, with a few gold bangles on each wrist, a gold bindi on her forehead, and a diamond stud on her left nostril

"Namaste! Erasmus has returned. It is so good to see you again." She got out of the chair and gave Erasmus a big hug.

"Neeru, yes, namaste. Thank you and Raj and everyone here for welcoming us to the Ashram. This is my grand-daughter, Aria, and our good friend, Mizz Joye."

Neeru turned to Aria, staring at her intently, with a surprised look. "Namaste, Aria. What a pretty name. What does it mean?"

"Namaste. So nice to meet you, Neeru," said Aria. She did a little curtsy and bowed with her hands together. "An aria is a melody, usually sung by just one voice, like in an opera. I've always loved my name. Wow, this Music Ashram is so amazing, thank you for allowing us to be here."

"Certainly, Aria. And I do love your purple hair," said Neeru. She was pondering something and looked again at Aria's hair. She then turned to Joye. "Mizz Joye, it is so nice to meet you. You are a powerful woman, I can tell."

"Namaste, Neeru. It's such a pleasure to be here. What can I say? I was just singing a song in Central Park and a few days later, I'm here in this magical place halfway around the globe. Life keeps on happening."

"Yes, it is something of a surprise that you all came so suddenly."

Erasmus said, "We're not entirely sure why we're here, but it was clear that we had to come."

Neeru looked at Aria. "Yes, I think we will soon find out. But now, let us have some dinner and then we can get together in the small music chamber over there."

Everyone staying at the ashram was at dinner. Some lived there, working at the ashram and teaching classes in music, meditation, dance, or yoga. Others were there for different periods of time for classes. Everyone seemed very chill.

Neeru introduced the newly arrived Americans, and they all enjoyed a delicious meal of rice, lentils, potato and cauliflower curry, some naan flatbread, and raita (which is a cucumber and yogurt side dish).

After dinner, Aria, Joye, Erasmus, Raj, and Neeru met in a small music room constructed of beautiful old wood. Aria sang a few notes. "Wow, how resonant."

They all sat down on lush pillows on the floor. "So, what brings you to the Devi Music Ashram?" asked Neeru.

They looked at one another, and Erasmus nodded for Aria to begin.

"Well, you see, I was asleep, and an angel came to me in a dream. I think it was a dream, and the angel said I was to bring peace to the world through fonging." Aria looked at Neeru to see her reaction, then continued. "The angel had come to my grandfather, Erasmus here, years ago. He wrote a book about fonging, but the angel said it's up to me now to fulfill the mission."

"What is this fonging?" asked Neeru. She was very interested in the conversation and was looking intently at her visitors.

"It's a little hard to describe," said Aria. She began to demonstrate in the air. "You really need to experience it. Basically, you take the rack out of your oven, tie two strings around the end, wrap the other end of the string around your fingers, lean over slightly from the waist, put your fingers in your ears, and people tap on the rack with various implements, and it makes this amazing sound in your head, which are in fact the healing sounds of the universe. The tappers and anyone watching can't really hear the sounds, only those with their fingers in their ears. I know, it seems weird, but it sounds amazeballs!"

"Hmm," said Neeru. "We'll have to try it."

Erasmus chimed in. "My feeling is that, by experiencing fonging and the healing sounds, fears, insecurities, and perceptions of separation can be reduced or eliminated. So, for example, after the angel came to Aria, just a couple days ago, she had a vision to go to New York. There, she found my old friend Mizz Joye, and they ran into Alexander Bozos, one of the richest men on earth."

"Alexander Bozos, of GOLIATH Enterprises?" asked Raj.

"Yes! And they fonged with him, and it seems his attitude about money changed instantly. When they left him in New York, he was thinking about transforming the old Trump Tower into a Music Ashram. How about that!"

Raj responded, "That is quite profound, indeed. More music ashrams are better."

"Then, I got on a holog with Aria and Mizz Joye from his condo. I called them, because I'd been hearing sitar music in my head, and turns out Aria had too, at the exact same time."

Aria continued, "And Bozos had this gold statue of Shiva in his condo, which mesmerized me, and when Bampa saw it on the holog, he immediately said, we've gotta go to Rishikesh. So, here we are."

Neeru thought, then asked, "And what effect do you think this fonging will have here in India?"

"I don't know," said Joye. "But the one thing that has struck me so far is there's so much deep spirituality here. Temples everywhere, so many statues of gods and goddesses. The aarti by the Ganga was amazing. But also such deep poverty, so much trash. And these people, the untouchables you call them, part of the caste system. It must be related to religion somehow, to Hinduism maybe. I don't know, since the spirituality here is off the charts, you'd think there'd be less poverty and suffering."

"That's a good point, Mizz Joye," said Erasmus. "Neeru,

is the caste system related to, or maybe caused by, religion?"

Neeru nodded her head. "Let me explain." She closed her eyes for a moment. "There are theoretically two caste systems in India."

"Two caste systems, whoa," said Aria, leaning into the conversation.

"There is the varna version of caste in ancient Hinduism," explained Neeru. "First, there is the Brahman level, which would be the scholarly people. Like philosophers, scientists, so that for example, Einstein would be a Brahman. Then, would be Shatriya, who would be soldiers and politicians, those who lead and protect the village or the country. Next are Vaishya, namely the business class; those who conduct the shops and companies. Finally, we have the Shudra, which are the laborers, the workers."

Raj added, "All of these categories have different characteristics and duties. The idea is that, if everyone does their duty, then all can achieve enlightenment. There is no conflict among the classes; no discrimination, but all in harmony."

Aria said, "It's like, if everyone does their job, then things will be cool."

"Yes," said Raj. "These classes are not based on birth, but on karma. One might also say that they are based on the passion a person has for life, what he or she wants to do with their life. It is perfectly fine to be a laborer, or a scientist. But this way, the needs of society are met by everyone doing their own thing, as you might say."

Neeru continued, "So, the theory of the system is beneficial for all. It is recognition of the value of everyone. But over the centuries, as empires changed, many selfish and greedy

men made the caste system into something more discrimina-
tory, and they used religion to bring to the people. This caste
system was called jaati. Now, this caste system depends on
birth class. Everyone in the higher castes is afraid to be in the
low caste, wants to be above the lower castes. No one wants
to be as low as the untouchables. Much suffering and cruelty
is coming from the discrimination of the castes."

Joye spoke up, "I believe what we've had in the United
States for so many centuries, really, is also a caste system.
The white people were the upper caste, especially the slave
owners, and the black enslaved people were the lowest caste.
Others could come along, like the European immigrants, who
were treated poorly but realized at least they weren't black.
So, they still had someone below them in their eyes. And it
seems many of the white people now, whose ancestors kept
my people down with unbelievable cruelty, still have this attitude and a deep fear of being the lowest caste."

"So," said Erasmus. "Maybe the healing sounds could
help people understand that these differences really celebrate
the richness of life. See that the fear of being a lower caste
is unwarranted. With such a strong spiritual resonance here
in India, and such a complex hierarchy, maybe we're here to
liberate or generate some particular sounds?"

Neeru was silent for a moment and then said, "Yes, I
think that is it. Now, I want to share something. Raj, can you
please bring out that trunk from back of the room. And, my
friends, I also must tell you some things about me."

Raj brought out a large wood container. He dragged it
over on a small carpet. It was old dark wood, with intricate
carvings of gods and goddesses, stars and planets, clouds

and waves, and swirls that seemed to vibrate. He dusted it off and sat down.

Neeru began. "My lineage goes back to the Rishis, several thousand years ago in India. You know of the Rishis? They were sages who possessed divine knowledge. They had the gift of inner vision and could see the past, present, and future. They were also scientists and were the scribes of the Vedas."

Aria asked, "So, that's how Rishikesh got its name?"

"Yes, Aria. My family line is not exactly written down; that was a long time ago to have records. But there are other things. I will tell you that my age is now two hundred and sixteen years."

Joye exclaimed, "Whoa, you have some good genes there, Neeru."

"Thank you, Mizz Joye. As with many Rishis, I simply stopped aging. I remember when it was. My mother performed a special puja when I was thirty-six, and I have not become older since then. A little gray hair sometimes." She laughed.

"Well, could you show me this puja, Neeru, please?" asked Joye with a grin.

Neeru laughed again and felt a special bond with Joye. "There is also much meditation, yoga, music, and development of third eye that leads to slowing of aging process. It is special and allows me to spend a long time appreciating life. But all my children have died, and my grandchildren are now seven generations. We don't talk about it too much. I am here, that is all."

"You have not aged since I met you years ago. I hadn't

really noticed. Remarkable," said Erasmus.

"Also, because of my line and lifestyle, I have been blessed with the fortune of sensory perception. I perceive many things with my senses. For example, your vibrational aura, I can perceive your colors, sounds, and even emotions and some of your past and future. I can say that you are each a beautiful shining note, and your future is bright."

"Wow, is that what's called synesthesia, Neeru?" asked Erasmus.

"Yes, I think that is the English name. I can only say, life is much more colorful and harmonious than most people appreciate."

Aria asked, "So, when someone says, 'heaven is every-where' or something like that, it literally is?"

Neeru laughed. "Yes, that is one way to put it. We are ex-isting in a cornucopia of beautiful vibration, color, and sound. Which brings me to you, Aria. And the reason I asked Raj to bring out this old box."

"Me?" asked Aria.

"This container, such beautiful wood and carvings, has been here for as long as I can remember. It comes through my family. The problem is, we cannot open it. It has Sanskrit written on it. Raj, can you read, please."

Raj got up and went over to the box. He touched it and ran his fingers across the writing. He read the inscription to himself, then looked at Aria. He closed his eyes and seemed to say a short prayer to himself. "This is very unusual. I read the Sanskrit, but it rhymes when I translate to English. Here is what it says:

They were speechless. Aria gasped. "Oh, my word. It's about me." How was this possible? She looked down, then at the box, and put her head in her hands. What was in the box?

Raj said, "I had never seen the word 'fong' before, and here it is on a box that is hundreds or maybe a thousand years old. Yet I am sure this is the correct translation."

Neeru said, "Aria. There is no way to understand how this has come to be. You have powerful karma. The gods and goddesses are looking on you brightly."

"What sort of key do I have? I don't have a key," whispered Aria.

"And what lair is being unlocked?" asked Erasmus.

"Maybe they mean the lair that can be human life? The brutal, cruel life that so many suffer. The blues. The untouchables, the enslaved," suggested Joye.

"Aria, please come over and feel this special old container. Listen to what your heart tells you about it," said Neeru.

Aria crawled over to the box, knelt next to it, and caressed it with her hands. She inspected and felt the carvings, the words, the ancient gods and goddesses. Her fingers followed every swirl. She closed her eyes and listened. Tears began to fall down her cheeks. She felt the power of the moment.

"I can hear it. I hear what's in this box. It's the most beautiful sound. It's like the healing sounds of fonging."

The others began to hear it too. The soft sounds were

definitely coming from inside the wooden trunk. But there was no lock or keyhole. It looked like a solid piece of wood. Even if she had a key, where would she put it?

Then, quietly, Aria said, "Does anyone have a turkey baster with them?"

Joye giggled out loud. "Aria, you're gonna open a thousand year old box with a turkey baster? Lordy. Well, what the heck, might as well give it a try!" There was something very serious yet comical about the situation. Erasmus volunteered to get the turkey baster he had from this luggage. While he was gone, they all touched and caressed the box, with the wonderous sounds emanating from it.

Erasmus returned and handed the turkey baster to Aria. They all got quiet. She felt around the box, and her hands came to a carved square symbol, with a circle inside and multiple triangles. It was right at the center of the front of the box.

"That is called shri yantra," said Neeru. "It is powerful Hindu symbol for the body of the goddess and the feminine shakti, which means energy."

Aria held her hand over it and said, "I feel it. This is the entry point." With that she closed her eyes, listened with her soul, and tapped the symbol with the turkey baster. Boof. "Open sesame," Aria cried out. That was all it took. The top of the box creaked and lifted off. They all stared.

"All I can say is, that's a bodacious turkey baster. What's inside?" asked Joye.

Aria gazed into the box. "I don't know what this is, but it's beautiful.

She reached in and pulled out what looked like a large

metal necklace, bedecked with jewels, diamonds, rubies, and sapphires. The metal was hard, and looked like brass. Attached to the thing were multicolored silk strands.

"What is it?" asked Joye.

"No idea," responded Aria. "But there are more in here. Three more. They're heavier than they look, but so beautiful." She tapped on it with the nail of her index finger. "Hmm, nice resonance."

"Oh, my lord," said Erasmus. "They're fonging racks! But much more elegant than oven racks; not even sure what to call them."

"Yes, I think you are correct, these are ancient fonging instruments," agreed Neeru.

"Well, I guess we should try them out," said Aria. "Since there are four of them, how would we do that?"

Erasmus said, "I'd go for a square fong, with four people all connected. One person in the middle doing the tapping."

"Check this out, there are silk strands linking them all together. Never saw that before," said Aria.

"Neither have I," said Erasmus.

Neeru suggested they take them outside to the main stage. Even though observers wouldn't hear the healing sounds, they could watch. This was quite a development and she thought it best to share with others. Aria and Joye carried the instruments very carefully to the outdoor amphitheater, and Raj and Erasmus managed to carry the box over. Then Raj spread the word to others at the Ashram.

When they were assembled, Neeru explained everything to them. There were a lot of oohs, aahs, and giggles as the story was told. Erasmus explained about fonging, and Aria told the story of fonging Alexander Bozos and how he had reacted.

"So," Neeru said. "I have known about the wooden box for a long, long time, but never knew what is was about. I did not know fonging. But it is clear the ancient Rishis, or whoever constructed the box, knew about fonging. And the fact that they put these fonging instruments into such a sacred container means it must be very special. Perhaps they were afraid the knowledge would be lost. In any event, this is the first time they will have been used in a very long time."

Aria then suggested, "There are four instruments, and they're connected, so how about Mizz Joye, Raj, Neeru, and me hold the racks and Bamps can sit in the middle and tap them? Let's see what we hear!"

The fonging instruments were stunning and even sensuous. Raj, Joye, Aria, and Neeru stood in a square facing one another, and each held one of the instruments. They got the feel of them, lightly wrapped the silk strands around their index fingers, leaned over slightly from the waist, and put their fingers in their ears. Erasmus sat on a small stool in the middle and began tapping.

He used various utensils and started tapping, softly and in various rhythms. He began to get into a groove, changing implements occasionally, building up to the turkey baster.

The four being fonged seemed to enter a trance-like state quickly. With eyes closed, they swayed nearly in unison, as if there was a cosmic beat underlying the healing sounds.

While the observers could barely hear the tapping, they all soon began to feel the vibrations. Erasmus could feel them, too. The healing sounds were emanating throughout the outdoor amphitheater. Everyone could now feel the sound, and they also began to enter into altered states. They were completely captivated by the sound, in sort of a Carnatic trance, like something the whirling dervishes experience.

The sound grew more intense. It was not a loud sound per se, but more of a sentient cloud of musical energy. Gradually, a diffused light built up in the amphitheater and it got rather bright, not as light, but again, as observable energy. Later, people said they could feel and see it from downtown Rishikesh on the other side of the Ganga River.

Finally, Erasmus slowed down and stopped tapping. It took everyone a few minutes to come out of it, like they were waking up. Those observing had a similar response.

"Oh. My. Life," exclaimed Aria. "That was incredible."

"You know it, those were some wild vibrations," said Joye.

Neeru said, "I could feel the healing sounds with all my senses. Not just hearing, sight, taste, touch, and sound, but also with my intuition. I believe that we experienced the Faad. The unstruck sound, the sound that is the underlying reality that creates the universe. Some say the Rishis could hear it; I believe we just did. We must give honor to this gift and play a song. Raj, can you please get your sitar and play with me?"

They put the ancient fonging instruments back in the box. Raj returned with his sitar.

Neeru said, "This is the favorite song of Mahatma Gandhi. It is a devotional song we call Bhajan. It is about empathy, love, equality, truth, and rejecting greed, lying, and evil."

Raj began playing his sitar and Neeru sang in Hindi.

Vaishnav jan to tene
Kahiye je. Peed parae jane re.
Par dukhe upkar kare toye,
Man abhiman na ane re.

Sakal lok maa sahune vande
Ninda naa kare keni re.
Vach kachh mann nishchal
Rakhe. dhandhan janani eni re.

Sam drishti neh trishna
Tyagi, parsti jane maat reh
Jivha thaki ashatha
Na bole, parhan naav
Jhali hath re.

Moh maya vyape nahi jane,
Dhridh vairagya jane,
Mann maan re.

The people in Rishikesh later said everything changed after that day. It was like the caste system had been dealt its death blow. Many gave money and clothing to the untouchables. There was a new societal resonance, like the tone of society had been changed, maybe as an old guitar that is finally restrung and tuned.

As they sat enjoying the music and the vibe of the Devi Music Ashram, Aria turned to Erasmus and said, "So, Bamps, now what are we going to do?"

CHAPTER FIVE

MUSIC OF THE TREES

After the amazing fonging experience at the Devi Music Ashram, they didn't have any plans. Everyone just needed to chill for a while and process what had happened.

So, they hung out at the Ashram. Sleeping, meditating, and playing music. They also took various classes in Indian music, such as singing, tabla, harmonium, and tanpura. Raj showed Joye how to play the sitar. Aria took classical India singing lessons with Neeru. Erasmus had fun talking with musicians there about some finer aspects of fonging and the healing sounds.

They had put the ancient fonging instruments back in the wooden box. No one could manage the energy to try that again soon. It had a profound and lasting impact though. Certainly, Aria, Joye, Neeru, and Raj – having actually fonged – had experienced something transformational. Such deep immersion into the healing sounds left them in a blissful state. How could one worry about or fear anything after essentially becoming one with the Faad?

A few days later, Erasmus received a call. It was an old friend he'd met on his first trip to the Devi Music Ashram. Sandro was a spiritual leader and guide from Brazil, who took seekers on trips to exotic places like India, the Australian outback, and to visit the shamans in the Amazon rainforests. His focus was on providing healing practices and music to those searching for peace.

"Namaste, Erasmus, my friend and brother. I saw on Artshare that you are in India; that is so nice, how is your trip?" said Sandro. Artshare was a new social medial platform supporting artists, musicians, and their fans and customers without ripping everyone off.

"Sandro, Namaste, how are you? So good to hear from you. Yes, we are at the Devi Music Ashram now. We've had an amazing time; it will take a while to tell you about everything. How are things in Brazil?"

Sandro said, "Not good, my friend. There are so many problems in the Amazon rainforest. We need help. I think you should come here. Soon."

Aria had come to listen to her grandfather regale everyone about fonging and heard Sandro. "Wow, the rainforests need help? What can we do?"

Erasmus said, "Sandro, this is my granddaughter Aria. Say hello to my good friend Sandro from Brazil, who I met here several years ago. He wanted my guitar."

"Yes, Erasmus, I still do want your guitar, it was such a nice one. Hello, Aria, nice meeting you. We do need help. I have listened to the animals and I can feel the trees and plants. The rainy season is not the same this year. Something is not good. So many people try to exploit the forests. I don't know why I call. I felt some deep vibrations the other day and thought of you, my brother. We need some strong healing for some new perspective about the dangers to the environment and this special part of the world. Can you come? We will go to the rainforests and make special ceremony."

"I don't think we have a choice, Bamps," said Aria. "Let's go."

* * * * * * *

It took a couple days to make the arrangements and then they were off to Brazil. Neeru decided to go with Aria, Joye, and Erasmus. Raj drove them to the airport, since he had business in Delhi.

"This may be crazy," said Joye, "but I don't think there are as many people begging on the streets as when we first got here."

"Maybe fonging does make a difference," said Erasmus.

"If we think it does, it will," said Aria.

"I believe you are right, Aria," said Raj.

It was a long trip to Sao Paulo, then to the town of Rio Branco in western Brazil in the Amazon, not far from Brazil's borders with Peru and Bolivia. There they met up with Sandro.

"Hello, my friend Erasmus, so good to see you," exclaimed Sandro with a big smile. He had long black hair and beard, and large dark glasses underneath a wide brimmed hat with a flowing white shirt. He also had a Brazilian wood guitar with him.

"Yes, Sandro, my brother. So good to see you. Please meet my granddaughter Aria, our friend Mizz Joye, and you know Neeru from the Devi Music Ashram." They all shared greetings.

Sandro said, "Thank you so much for coming all the long way. When I sense your vibrations the other day, it was combined with a strong worry feeling about the environment, especially here in the rainforests of Brazil. This is such a special place, as you will learn. We will rest here for overnight, then go by small boat to visit the village of the Huni Kuin tribe in the rainforest."

They got themselves ready for the four-hour boat trip the next day and talked while relaxing. Aria told Sandro all about fonging, their encounter with Alexander Bozos, and the fongtabulous experience at the Devi Music Ashram with Neeru. Sandro also told them more about the rainforest.

The Amazon River Basin is huge, covering forty percent of South America. The Amazon is considered the largest river in the world, and only the Nile River in Egypt is longer in length. The Amazon rainforest is also the largest in the world - ten times the size of Spain – and is not confined just to the Amazon River Basin, extending much more broadly. Many call this large area Amazonia, comprised mostly of Brazil, but also Columbia, Venezuela, Bolivia, Guyana, Suriname, Ecuador, and French Guiana.

Amazonia has something like 400 billion trees, which each exhale incredible amounts of water. Trees literally create rain. The humidity in the rainforests is very high and results in enormously productive and diverse plant and animal ecosystems. The trees grow very high; for example, the kapok tree can grow over 200 feet tall!

The rainforests also feature lianas, woody vines that grow by climbing up on trees, then branching out and forming networks among the trees far above the forest floor. They form a canopy that can be more than 100 feet high, 30 feet thick, and prevents most sunlight from reaching the ground. As a result, it is quite dark and wet on the forest floor.

Sandro told them about many plants and animals of the rainforest. "I have learned almost half of the plant and animal species in the world are here in the rainforest. There are about 1500 bird species, so many types of incredible birds. The strange stinkbird, the laughing falcon, and lots of hummingbirds. Frogs, lizards, many different types, no one knows how many. There are lots and lots of kinds of fish in the rivers, including the ruthless pirana. They say one river may have more species of fish than all the rivers of Europe combined. Many types of monkeys, bats that drink blood, even human blood, and poisonous snakes, too."

"Tell me why we are going deep into the rainforest again, please," asked Joye.

"You will love it, Mizz Joye. It is so important we go and bring the healing sounds to support the environment here. The Amazon rainforest is so much critical to the health of the world. Many problems are here, deforestation is really doing much damage to all of the life, including the indigenous peoples. We will see more tomorrow." They played a few songs and talked for a while, then all went to bed to get some sleep before their journey.

The next morning, Sandro drove them in a twenty-foot flat bottomed wood boat, with its sides only ten inches above the water. He continued to tell them about the rainforest.

"Our peoples in South America arrive here over 10,000 years ago and learn the ways of the forest. They live with nature and have much gratitude for all the plants and animals in the forest. They all live together and our peoples they respect the forest. But, you may know this, the Europeans came in the 1500s and they take everything. They are the conquistadors from Spain, Portugal, England, and other countries in Europe, and they murder the people and make them slaves. The diseases they bring also kill many, many peoples. They take away our history and our culture, like in the United States."

Erasmus chimed in, "I remember in history class learning about some of the explorers, you know, after Columbus. We thought they were brave and virtuous, but that wasn't true. Francis Drake was really a ruthless pirate who stole and plundered for Queen Elizabeth. They were blood thirsty, cruel, and greedy men. They murdered and enslaved many native people."

"South America had huge amounts of gold and silver from the mountains and the Europeans stole as much as they could. So much that it changed the economies of Europe with all that new wealth," said Sandro.

"So terrible," sighed Aria. "Seems like the same stories all over the world. Why do humans treat each other so badly?"

Neeru said, "We can make a change in the consciousness. I do see that in the future."

"What's that over there? Is that a crocodile? Oh my, tell me he's not coming after us." Aria clutched the side of the boat and stared across the river.

"That is the black caiman, like a crocodile. It eats everything, snakes, armadillos, deer, fish, monkeys, so powerful,"
replied Sandro. "Let's sing a sweet song for our protection."

Aria began a song with her best intentions. The caiman
slowly turned and headed the other direction.

"Nice Aria, perfect," whispered Joye. "Maybe you can also
sing up some beautiful birds and they can cheer us along our
way."

Aria began singing a new verse, and immediately a flock
of brightly colored macaws flew over them and landed on the
muddy river bank. The macaws had blue wings, with red and
yellow face and body feathers. Several green billed toucans
also hopped from tree to tree along the shore.

"Oh, I just love the birds, so beautiful," said Erasmus,
peering across the water. "Look at the green songbirds over
there," he pointed. "And all the butterflies!" As if called by
Aria's voice, hundreds of multi-colored butterflies also appeared and flew across the river, over their heads, and to the
trees on the other side. "This is a magical place."

"It is remarkable, but what we come to the rainforest for,"
said Sandro, "is the wisdom of the plants. The plants are
most important because they give life to all the animals. The
indigenous people they learn all about the plants and how
they also heal people when they have problems. The shamans of the Huni Kuin will explain to you."

A couple hours later, having been escorted and serenad-
ed by a variety of birds along the way, they arrived at the town
of the shamans. Duabu Sam and his wife Irani greeted them
as they got off the boat, walking down a wooden plank from
the village on higher ground.

"Greetings, Sandro, thank you for coming," called out Duabu Sam. He was tall, with dark beard and braided hair, wearing a tee-shirt with a picture of a green spirit on the front. Irani, adorned in colorful native dress with feathers, came over to Sandro and gave him a big hug. "So nice to see you, my friend, and welcome to your guests."

"Hello, Duabu Sam and Irani. These are my special friends to meet you. Aria, with the purple hair, her grandfather Erasmus, their friend Mizz Joye, and mutual friend Neeru from India." Sandro had a big grin as he introduced them. Neeru also was smiling; evidently, she perceived goodness in their hosts.

They said their hellos and Irani showed them around and to their huts with brown grass thatched roofs. Irani said, "Please rest and get ready for the ceremony tonight. We will see you soon."

The skies began to cloud up as they gathered in the main building. It had a porch overlooking the river, with trees all around and a mountain in the distance.

"It is the wet season, so you have good luck on your trip, but we may have some rain soon," said Irani.

A little later, they congregated for the ceremony. There was a glowing fire in the center of the main room, and a few musicians played drums and shakers. There were colorful paintings and statues all around the room. It felt like home. Aria, Joye, Erasmus, and Neeru found chairs or large pillows to sit and listen. Duabu Sam tended the fire as he talked.

"Welcome to our family, the Huni Kuin tribe. There are hundreds of tribes in the Amazon, many have not been contacted by outsiders. Irani and I are shamans, each of us seven generations of this spiritual practice in the rainforest. Our family members who will be assisting with the ceremonies, they are also shamans who will help you. We listen to the plants, and they tell us secrets of how to live. They tell us which plants can help and heal us of our problems, whether physical, mental, or spiritual. As shamans, we see the interconnectedness of all things."

Duabu Sam continued, "Our friend Sandro told us about feeling your vibrations from halfway across the world. You have created powerful healing sounds. We thank you for that."

"We're just making this up as we go along," said Aria. "We're literally just following the vibrations, a mystical resonance of some type. We don't know. Fonging has an impact on an individual level, as music does, but also on a collective level."

"It sure does, and I'm surprised by what happened in New York and India," added Joye. "There is something to this fonging stuff. Now, how can we help here in the Amazon?"

Sandro spoke up, "Of this, I am not exactly sure. But I trust in the healing sounds. I felt the power of the vibrations from fonging thousands of miles away. These sounds connect us. And what we are facing is so critical. The indigenous peoples have been living and hunting and acting as stewards here for thousands of years, but they are in danger."

Duabu Sam was still reverently tending the fire. Everyone was very chilled out. This hut had a special vibe. Sandro continued, "The Amazon rainforest actually helps the world to breathe. Changes here affect all around the planet. But a fifth of the rainforest has been cut in the last forty years. Yes, sadly, that is true. And where the indigenous people have been removed, deforestation is worse. If we lose the rainforest, it will be like losing the skin of the earth."

Neeru said, "This valuable ecosystem of the rainforest must be helped, and we can devote our intentional vibration to that purpose. It must be powerful. I can see that you all are knowing of the spirit world from the plants. We must learn from the spirit of earth, with Pachamama. How is it best to do that?"

"We make the ceremonies, for the water and the fire, and we learn from Mother Ayahuasca through the plant medicine. That is what we must do," said Duabu Sam.

"If you think the plants can help, I'm in," said Aria.

The others agreed. Joye said, "I don't know what I'm getting myself into, but why not at this point?"

Erasmus agreed, "All for one and one for all, right?"

Irani explained that they would do a water ceremony first, to pay homage to the rivers and the rain that brings life. Then, a ceremony in thanks for fire, which allows humans to live comfortably. The people living in the jungle express deep gratitude for the blessings of nature.

"We will do some chanting and praying to begin," said Irani. "We will use plant medicines. As shamans, we see the connection between the physical world and the spiritual world. These plants put us in touch with the spirits. We use many plants for healing in different ways. The plants tell us what they can do. Ayahuasca is called the vine of the soul. We in the Amazon have used it for thousands of years. It helps to see our lives as connected, and to clarify our purposes with clear eyes. First, we shall drum out some dark spirits and memories, cleansing the soul. Then, the plant medicine will help you feel oneness. We often see the future, and sometimes change the past."

Music was an integral part of the ceremonies, which Duabu Sam and Irani now initiated. They each lit a large roll-up made of mountain herbs and puffed on it. They both went around and blew smoke on each of the fongsters; on their heads, on their skin, all over. Praying and exhorting the spirits to help these humans, and ward off dark spirits.

Sandro chanted while Duabo Sam prayed in honor of the water, paying homage to the liquid energy that comes up from the earth and falls out of the sky to sustain life. Irani sang and celebrated the fire, the light of the world, the heat, the source from the sun and the stars.

The ceremonies continued and, about an hour later, Duabu Sam took a bottle with a dark liquid from the shelf. It had been brewing in a large pot for 12 hours. It's made from the ayahuasca vine and leaves of the chacuna plant. The plants work together to allow the spirits to communicate with humans and open them to all possibilities.

Duabu Sam poured a cup of the liquid for the five of them. "You would do good to think about and direct your intentions for this journey." Each of them closed their eyes and thought of what they wanted, then drank their portions.

"It sure doesn't taste very good," said Aria.

"You got that right, Aria. I've had some nasty things to drink in my life, and this is one of them," added Joye.

They sat still and let the plant medicine do its magic.

Aria thought, "I'm so grateful for this experience with my grandfather and my new friends. Already I've changed in ways

I could never have conceived. This fonging stuff is so crazy, but the healing vibrations are powerful. I want to do my best to have peace of mind for myself, to be happy, whole, and free, loved and loving, and bring peace to the world through fonging, or however I can. How did I come to this? Is it insane?"

About twenty minutes later, she began seeing colors, fractals, moving designs, planets, and flowers. Then, her head began to spin and she felt nauseous. Soon, she was purging a fluorescent yellow liquid and green geckos! She felt awful. Recalling her youth, she saw her mama and papa, and felt intense love and appreciation. Now a pang of guilt, as she remembered constantly badgering her little brother, from the time he was an infant, taking his toys, then as an adult, sneakily getting him into trouble. She cried. Extremely willful as a child, Aria learned how to get her way. She sometimes didn't consider others' feelings or desires. She cried at her lack of empathy. She knew she'd become better, but the spirit of the plant was forcing her to look at her past.

The rain started, and grew heavier, thunder too, until the water pounded the roof in torrents, and guilt wracked her heart. She sobbed.

Her first music teacher's face popped up in front of her. He was so nice, until he was berating her for missing a note, losing the beat, not understanding how to make a chord. She was young, but it almost derailed her desire to play music. For some time, when playing, she became terrified of how she would sound, if she made a mistake. It took the fun out of music, stole the spontaneity out of her playing. It was her grandfather's joy in bringing different instruments around that kept her into music. The rain fell even harder.

Finally, a speck of blue light. It grew and she realized it was the earth, the amazing blue ball of life hanging in the middle of space. Her perspective then zoomed to the Amazon rainforest. She saw trees, lianas, monkeys, parrots, butterflies, and then realized they were all crying. They were burning from the inside. The planet was on fire. She watched her grandfather and her family and friends, every human, burn as if staked, then incinerated. Life wafted up and away from the land and the oceans, and soon there were no living things left. No color, no sound, no light or life. She was in pitch darkness again. Alone. She cried out in agony. She would die.

She felt Irani touch her shoulder, wave a straw brush in the air, on her shoulders, then in a steady rhythm. Irani communicated telepathically, "You are fine. You are sound and light. Be patient."

She could hear the musicians playing. The rain let up. The music soothed her, a purple sun rose and a flock of white birds flew by, their wings beating in time. The sky of her mind brightened, and all of a sudden, the deepest feeling of gratitude she ever experienced washed over her. She became empathy, then joy, elation, intoxication, wholeness.

She lost all sense of self and became everything and nothing at the same time. She now cried for joy, tears streaming down her face, every pore of her nonexistent body smiling. She had no boundaries and could not die. There was no separation. No fear. She became one with the universe, and it was pure bliss and love.

"Aria." A heavenly feminine voice whispered to her. Was this the angel again? No.

"Aria, I am your mother."

Her mother? No, not her human mother. All of a sudden, she realized, she knew. Mother Earth was talking with her!

"Yes, Mother," replied Aria. She was completely blissed out. She'd never felt this possible. Mother Earth was a conscious, living entity. Aria was communicating with her somehow. But were they even communicating in words?

"I am the spirit of the earth, as you are the spirit of your body. I feel you, I know what you are doing. Thank you."

"Thank me, wow! I mean, you're Mother Earth. Everything I know, everywhere I've been, is you. Jeepers." Aria knew she was still affected by the ayahuasca, but she also knew this was real.

"By the way," said Mother Earth, "The healing sounds of fonging are very nurturing."

Aria felt some sort of indescribable warmth. Mother Earth was giving her a spiritual hug!

"Oh, thank you so much, Mother." Aria realized she needed to think practically. What did she need to say to Mother Earth? This doesn't happen every day. Or does it?

Aria asked, "What can we do to help you, Mother Earth? I know humans have been terrible to you and to the land, water, plants, and animals. What should we do?"

"Many of you don't understand the unity of all things in nature. With your limited perspective of separation, many fall victim to greed and selfishness. It seems it can be difficult to change your consciousness. But what you are doing right now, bringing the healing sounds of fonging, is very helpful. Keep it up. I will be fine. For humans, it's up to you."

Aria couldn't see Mother Earth, but only felt her presence

as a cool breeze and vibrations.

Mother Earth said, "Fong on, Aria. Know that I will always be with you. Now, you must become one with the trees to accomplish your goals. Also, don't forget to ask the Spirit of Music for help whenever you need it."

Suddenly, Aria became a purple liquid. Where was she? It felt as though she was descending through something porous – wood! She was tree sap, and apparently heading down to the roots!

"Why am I blue liquid?" cried out Joye.

"Oh, Mizz Joye, so great to, uh, see you? Are you blue paint?"

"I don't know, child, this is some hell of a medicine. And what are you? Not just purple hair, you're purple paint too!"

"I think we're tree sap, and we're headed to the roots!" called out Aria as the noise of the root chakra increased.

"Why are you two blue and purple," asked Erasmus. "Oh, wait, I'm orange. Yikes!"

"This is the most incredible experience of the senses," said Neeru. "Synesthesia is nothing compared to being tree sap!" Neeru was golden.

"Namaste, my friends, so glad to be with you. How is your journey?" Sandro was liquid green.

"Well, at least we're all together. Let's see where this tree is taking us, whoa!" cried out Aria.

They started in a circular motion around the tree, down to the roots. "It's gonna be dark down here," called out Erasmus.

But it wasn't dark. The darkness turned to colored lights!

"How can it be so bright here in the ground?" asked Joye.

Neeru replied telepathically, "Animals and plants perceive

differently than humans. Dogs and many other animals hear much better than we do. Many animals see differently, too. They see lights we don't see, frequencies we can't hear. We're seeing the way mycelia perceive life under the earth."

They had flowed along with the roots to the mycelia, the fungal network having a symbiotic relationship with plants. Plants provide the fungi with food, carbohydrates, and the fungi help the plants by returning nutrients. Mycelia are crucial for plant growth and health of the soil, and for millions of years created the conditions for other life on the planet.

The multicolored retinue surged along faster now, through narrow tentacles around rocks and roots, moving faster underground. Where were they going?

"The mycelia network is all over the world. It's like a fungal internet," called out Sandro. "It feels like we're moving very fast!"

They began to perceive what was above ground, as their subterranean journey continued. They realized they were headed north, under the Amazon, up through Central America, around and under the Mississippi River, and toward New York.

Then, they heard a sound like a high-pitched drone.

"I recognize that sound," said Erasmus telepathically, "It's the cicadas, the seventeen-year locusts we call them. They come up out of the ground every seventeen years for about three weeks. But this is not their year."

"I sense the cicada larvae in the ground as we are passing by," added Neeru.

"Sweet Mother," cried out Aria, "I think we're hearing their future sounds!"

"Holy smokes," cried Erasmus, "I'm feeling the three cedar trees at the Namaste Music Ashram, and Queen Sycamore, the tree I planted there. I love those trees!" He began to weep tears of joy.

They continued their journey, westward across Canada, under the Bering Strait using ancient mycelial pathways, over to Europe, the Middle East, around Africa, and through India, China, and returning down the western United States to exactly where they started. They began to go up the same exact kapok tree. It slurped them skyward along with the xylem sap; slurp, slurp, slurp.

Soon, they were near the top of the tree. "Let's blow this pop stand," called out Aria. They exited as respiration through the pores of leaves and found themselves hanging on to branches about one hundred feet above ground.

Joye said, "I think I've got my body back, I'm not sap anymore. Right on!"

"Me, too," said Aria, "I can see all of you, I think."

"What are we going to do way up here?" asked Erasmus. He was frantically grasping some branches and large lianas for stability.

"We should not pray for rain, maybe," suggested Sandro.

"I know," called out Aria. "Mother Earth told me to remember to ask the Spirit of Music for help. Let's do that?"

"You were talking with Mother Earth? Don't that beat all," said Joye. "You are a special girl, that's for sure."

Aria sang out:

Spirit of Music, hear us please.
We're at the top of some very tall trees!
Spirit of Music, hear us please.
Hear us, hear us, hear us, please.

The wind began to blow in rhythms, the trees swaying in time, and countless leaves clapped along.

"Aria, I hear you. I am the Spirit of Music. You and your fellow musicians help me all the time by allowing me to express music through you. I need you, just like you need your voice and your instruments to play. How can I help you now?" Her voice sailed on the wind.

"Oh, Spirit of Music, thank you," replied Aria. "We're on a mission to bring peace to the world through fonging. We're just making it up as we go along, but how can we help the rainforest with the healing sounds?"

"I think we're gonna need some powerful fonging to help this gigantic forest," injected Joye.

"Can we use the lianas somehow?" asked Erasmus.

"You are an intrepid group, I'll give you that," said the Spirit of Music. "Here, try out this large gong."

Suddenly, a huge bronze gong appeared, and the lianas reached out and suspended it high off the ground. It was hanging from the vines between the trees, swinging in the breeze as if ready to sound.

"That's the biggest gong I've ever seen, it's way taller than you, Aria," shouted Joye.

"What are we gonna hit it with?" asked Aria.

"Here you go," called the Spirit of Music, and a large mallet appeared in Aria's hands. It was golden with padded heads.

"How am I supposed to hit it from way over here?" shouted Aria. She was trying to balance one hundred feet above the forest floor with the heavy mallet.

"Trust the lianas, Aria. The plants will help you," called out Sandro.

"Alrighty then, here we go." Aria dove off into the air and the vines grabbed her around the ankles and flung her toward the giant gong. She took a big backswing and hit the gong slightly off center as she flew by. BONG! She ricocheted back and swung the mallet again, BONG!

It was the deepest most resonant sound they'd ever heard. It reverberated through the air; you could see the sound waves as colors of the rainbow as they emanated outward like ripples on a pond. The lianas began to vibrate too, slowly and then faster, more strongly, reverberating with the trees, and the whole forest began to vibrate.

It was like an earthquake of sound. Outward the vibrations went, into the sky, down the trees, into the roots, speeding along the mycelial network underground, through all parts of the world. A surge of healing sounds above and below the ground circumnavigated the globe.

Several shamans from the past and future floated up in the air and, hovering, blew darts with pinpoint accuracy right at the gong. A melody began, like rainfall on a tin pan, and the higher tones punctuated the atmosphere, sending the healing sounds to far-flung regions of the world.

"Can you see this?" cried Neeru. "Sounds and colors

throughout the entire aural and visual palette! Can you taste it, sense it on your skin? Can you feel the vibrations in your heart, in your soul?"

"Yes, yes!" Erasmus was dancing in the air, uplifted by woody lianas.

"The trees are playing music, they're shaking it too," added Joye. She was perched over one hundred feet off the ground in a hammock of vines, swinging with the primal vibrations.

"Aria, I think the trees have something to say to us," said Sandro. He was sitting side saddle on some vines.

The trees definitely had something to say. Since they don't have mouths or vocal cords, they communicate by floral sensations.

We represent all plants of the earth and thank you for your healing vibrations. Your species is in desperate need of this healing. We as plants feed this world. We take air, sunlight, water, and soil, and we create ourselves and food for everything else on the planet through the chain of nutrition. We are your homes and furniture, fences and electric poles, boats and bats, and fuel and paper.

Yet, we want nothing. We give what we are and what we have created for you to live, and so you can be grateful, to understand as the first peoples did, that all of nature is a gift to be thankful for. We are creators as you are, contributors. The shamans understand this, they know us, how we evolved with one another.

But many of you have learned the economy of fear, to take as much as you can. It is a foolish pursuit. It results in unneces-

sary destruction and degradation of the holiness of the planet. To what end? The indigenous peoples here and around the world understand the gifts they receive, and how gratitude makes them important.

Humans now risk the sustainability of their lives and their earth home. If they cannot understand oneness, that we are all part of and inextricably tied to one another, humans shall perish, with countless species of plants and animals, a slaughter caused by your greed.

Still, we have hope, and we have faith in you, and we thank you. These healing sounds have been felt around the world by our family of trees, plants, weeds, flowers, fungi, and roots. We have sensed your nurturing intentions. We are with you, supportive of the mission you have undertaken. We shall play our own music. Know that we shall support you everywhere you go because we are grateful for you. We see the same light and love of you in us. We are all the same. Namaste.

Aria opened her eyes. She looked around and saw her grandfather lying on some cushions on the ground, almost like he was just watching television. Mizz Joye had a smile on her face as she laid in a hammock. A hammock? How was that possible? Had they really been there with her?

Neeru's eyes opened and she looked at Aria. "I feel as if all the trees in the world just thanked us for fonging. That was most unusual."

"Neeru, they did, you all were there, weren't you? You were sap with me, right?" asked Aria.

Neeru laughed. "I don't know about any sap. I had an amazing experience, and I have this sensation of trees vibrating and being grateful."

Sandro stretched his arms as he came out from the effects of the medicine. "Oh, wow, that was so amazing! I am feeling wholeness with everything. And I did have a feeling listening to the music of the trees. But, no sap."

Aria shook her head. "We fonged the trees way up high with a huge bronze gong held up by lianas."

They stared at her.

"Well," Aria said, "I think somehow the trees did experience the healing sounds."

"For sure, they did," said Erasmus, yawning. "That was an incredible experience. I don't remember any sap either, but I did travel super-fast underground somehow, all over the world. I heard cicadas. And felt the cedar trees at our Music Ashram. That was so bizarre."

"Bamps, that's what I did too! The mycelia networks! It all just blew my mind."

Joye said, "I felt like I was traveling underground part of the time, too. It was so beautiful, the entire experience. I am very grateful for the plant medicine, too."

Duabu Sam had been listening, and now spoke. "From my observation and my experience, it seems as though the plant medicine was very good for all of you. And sometimes people can share experiences while with the medicine. The experience is not necessarily the most important thing. It is what have you learned from the plants. What has your spirit learned? What will you do now? How will you help heal others?"

Irani added, "The ayahuasca medicine is from plants, so it is not unusual to feel the reality of the plants. Aria, your experience was very dramatic. I watched and felt. Your powerful vision of fonging the trees was impactful."

"It was so powerful, but we were over a hundred feet in the air so it was just insane, impossible. But it felt real." Aria took a breath and smiled. "And what I learned is that we're all connected, and we can all help one another. I felt whole, as if there's no separation between anything, no self. And I gained new reverence for the plants, the trees. This trip is totally worth it."

"What an experience," said Erasmus. "It will take a while to think through this. In the meantime, Sandro, would you play us a song to celebrate such good medicine, please?"

"Yes, sure," said Sandro. "I hope you like this song; it is from the indigenous peoples of the Andes. Pachamama means Mother Earth."

Pachamama, I'm coming home
To the place where I belong

I wanna be free so free
Like a feather blowing through the breeze
Like a bird in a tree
Like a dolphin in the sea

I wanna fly high so high
Like an eagle in the sky
And when my time has come
I'll let it all go and Fly

Pachamama, I'm coming home
To the place where I belong

Pachamama, I'm coming home
To the place where I belong

I wanna be free, be me
Be the only being that I see
Not to rise and not to fall
Be at one with love and all

There is no high, no low
There is nowhere else to go
Except inside within your heart
And be just who you are

Pachamama, I'm coming home
To the place where I belong
Pachamama, I'm coming home
To the place where I belong.

They all clapped when he was done. Aria had been quietly listening to the song, but seemed distant. Then she covered her mouth in horror.

"Oh, oh, Bamps," said Aria. "I had another vision." She wrinkled her face and looked up.

"What did you see?" asked Erasmus.

"Some men in dark suits, wearing headphones with red lights. They were assaulting the United States Capitol, just like the Insurrection. But not with poles, flags, or guns. I think they were doing something that dimmed the lights at the Capitol. I think we should find out what's happening. They might need some healing sounds."

"Oh, boy," said Joye. "Here we go again."
Sandro said, "I'm coming too!"

CHAPTER SIX

THE MUSIC ACT

The United States Capitol, a beacon of freedom across the world, stood bright in the twilight. It looks toward the setting sun across the National Mall, past the Washington Monument, and to the Lincoln Memorial. Such an inspiring sight!

But as the twilight turned to dark, the lights of the Capitol dimmed and went out! The majestic dome turned dark. Those walking along the Mall, around the Congressional office buildings, and the nearby neighborhoods gasped audibly. What in the world?

Congressman Hoyez Jazzkin of the great state of Maryland was in his office in the Rayburn House Office Building when the lights dimmed. Dressed in white shirt and tie, with his sleeves rolled up, he saw it from the window. What puzzled him more was that the music playing from his wireless speaker also went silent.

Jazzkin was the main Congressional sponsor of the MUSIC Act – Musicians United in Support of Instrumental Communities, which was soon to be debated on the floor of the House of Representatives. Jazzkin played piano and was also the chair of the House Music Caucus, which had been working on the legislation for six months. There was opposition from some business and conservative groups, so the Caucus was working hard to pin down support from legislators.

When the lights and music went back on a minute later, Jazzkin was relieved, but curious. He would ask the Capitol Police about it, hoping nothing sinister was going on.

In front of the Library of Congress, three men in dark suits wearing headphones with blinking red lights hurried away.

* * * * * *

It took our intrepid crew of fongsters a few days to make their way back from Brazil. They stayed for a couple more ceremonies, which cemented their beliefs in the power of plant medicine. Sandro led them back down the river and to the airport. After the long grueling flights to Washington, DC, they all needed some crash time at the Namaste Music Ashram. They slept, took walks along the river, and played music. Neeru and Sandro had never been to the United States, so they were delighted to visit and wanted to tour the nation's capital.

Erasmus suggested they go to downtown DC at night to see the sights. Aria, Joye, Neeru, and Sandro piled in the car and Erasmus drove. From the Ashram, it was an easy drive down Canal Road after rush hour. They went along the Whitehurst Freeway, the Rock Creek Parkway past the Kennedy Center, and then Ohio Drive, where they parked just south of the Lincoln Memorial, a short distance from the Potomac River.

"I just loved the way the Kennedy Center was all lit up with the rainbow colors," said Joye. "It's nice when people recognize our diversity in such a beautiful way."

"It is such a great view along the river there," added Sandro. "Quite a fascinating city."

Erasmus led them across West Potomac Park to the Martin Luther King, Jr. Memorial on Independence Avenue next to the Tidal Basin. The memorial was all lit up.

"This is so inspiring," said Joye, "No matter how many times I've seen this, it just keeps getting better. I have my sheroes, but MLK meant so much to us. This is stunning."

There weren't too many visitors, as it was early March and chilly outside with a light northwest wind. The waxing moon rose over the mall and lit up the Jefferson Memorial.

"Memorials to a slave owner President and the man who helped get the Civil Rights Act passed, right across the Tidal Basin from one another. What a history we've had," said Joye.

"I went to UVa and we revered Jefferson," said Erasmus. "The things he did, Virginia statute of religious freedom, author of the Declaration of Independence, and such a smart man. I mean, all men created with inalienable rights, that's powerful stuff."

"Yea, Bamps, all *men* created equally." Aria walked over and gave her grandfather a hug. "But we've come a long way baby."

"Yes, the United States has been a guide for democracy around the world," added Neeru. "In my country, too. Gandhi was our hero, like your Martin. The atmosphere here is so uplifting. I can see trust in the air. It has a certain hue."

"Wow, that's cool, Neeru," agreed Aria. "I love that we're

down here at night, with the moon, and the monuments lit up. It's always been inspiring to me. There's something about the Mall. It makes you feel patriotic, and reminds you that we're all part of this democratic country. It's ours."

"Well, like Aria said, it hasn't been for everyone, with the long history of slavery and discrimination in voting rights," said Joye. "But I agree it's inspiring. We can keep striving for that more perfect union."

"I think trust is the cornerstone of democracy," said Erasmus. "Interesting that Neeru can perceive it visually. Everyone gets to vote and participate. That's the way it has to be for democracy to succeed. The effort to destroy trust that happened when we were also dealing with the pandemic almost brought us down. Hey, I know a really inspiring spot; let's walk over to the Lincoln Memorial."

They walked across Independence Avenue with the breeze in their face, and up the grand steps to the giant statue of Abraham Lincoln. After gazing at Honest Abe, they turned around and from the top step looked down the National Mall.

"This is amazing, my friends," said Sandro. "I feel what is like to be American right now."

"Taj Mahal does not even compare," added Neeru. "It's just a gaudy tomb. This vision represents the soul of a nation."

The view is spectacular. Looking across the reflecting pool, with the bright Washington Monument image mirrored in the water, then across another fifteen city blocks to the Capitol. Museums and federal government offices lined the Mall. All the buildings were lit up.

Erasmus got a little teary-eyed. He hugged his granddaughter. "It's our home," he said. He reached over and hugged Joye, too. "I think the ideals of equality and democracy are worth fighting for, don't you think, my dear friend?"

"Land of the free and home of the brave; supposed to be any way," replied Joye. "It's worth the fight for all of us to be free."

"The whole world around, Mizz Joye," said Aria, also hugging Joye.

Sandro said, "Hey, we want some of this hugging, too." He and Neeru joined an impromptu group hug, as they gazed out at the view.

All of a sudden, the lights of the Capitol and those shining up at the Washington Monument dimmed, flashed, and then went out. They gasped.

The tourists were stunned into silence. The lights of the Reflecting Pool and the Lincoln Memorial were still on. A few police officers started to run toward the Capitol, but stopped when they realized they didn't know what to do.

"This is what I saw, Bamps, but it was only the Capitol lights. Now it's the Washington Monument too. What's going on?"

Then, the lights flickered and came back on.

"Something is really weird," exclaimed Joye. "What do we do?"

"Well," offered Erasmus. "Let's walk to the Capitol and see what we can see. We can go by the Vietnam Memorial on the way; it's amazing."

It was a long walk, but they all enjoyed the brisk night. The Vietnam Memorial is so profound; a deep, dark gash in the ground, exposing the emptiness of war. As they walked toward the Capitol, Sandro asked, "What's that building over there, that looks like flowing rock?"

Erasmus responded, "That's the National Museum of the American Indian. It's beautiful, made of limestone on the outside. It was designed with help from many Native Americans."

"And here's something else," added Aria. "The Iroquois Confederacy was a model for democracy used by our founding fathers in designing our government. I learned that in class."

It was true. In 1142, the Great Peacemaker and Hiawatha brought five warring Indian nations together from what is now the Northeastern United States and Canada into a governance agreement, known as the Great Law of Peace. The tribes were equal, had specific roles and responsibilities, and determined matters of joint interest together. Their name in the native language was Haudenosaunee, the people of the longhouses.

They developed layers of governance to peacefully address issues based on the communal living model of many families in a single longhouse. They had local village councils, nation councils, and finally the Grand Council of Chiefs. Their decision-making was based on consensus; unanimity was required. Everyone could speak in the meetings and, when done, they would all wait in silence for a few minutes to make sure the speaker didn't have anything else to say.

Aria continued, "It was an elaborate governance system that Ben Franklin learned about and held up as a model when the founders were writing the Declaration of Independence and the Constitution. Interesting, the tribes were matrilineal, with descent based on the female line, rather than the male, and with the Clan Mothers having the ultimate authority to select or remove the chiefs."

Joye piped up, "Maybe that's a feature we should reconsider."

"Yes, I think you are correct, Mizz Joye," laughed Neeru.

When they finally got to the Capitol, they didn't see anything amiss. Being up close to that colossal dome at night, when all lit up, is powerful. It was hard to imagine that some people once stormed the Capitol and wanted to execute lawmakers.

Neeru said, "There is some dark energy somewhere around here."

Erasmus said, "I have an idea. Tomorrow I'll call our Congressman; he's a friend of mine. I'll see if he knows anything."

It took a while to get back to the car, but they all felt it was good to really stretch their legs. The moon made it almost like daylight, so it was easy to see. They were tired on the ride home and didn't talk much, pondering the cause of the lights going out.

The next day, Erasmus rang up a holog with Congressman Jazzkin, who represented the district where the Music Ashram was located. "I have his personal contact info," he confided to the group.

"Hello," answered Representative Hoyez Jazzkin. The image of Erasmus popped up in 3-D in front of Jazzkin.

"Hello, Congressman, this is your old friend, Erasmus Caffery. From the Namaste Music Ashram. How are you? You're looking fit as a fiddle!" Jazzkin also was in holographic form before Erasmus.

"Ah, yes, Erasmus, great to see you. I know you're always up to something interesting!"

"We've had an amazing month traveling around the world; I'll tell you about it sometime. But I wanted to call you because we were downtown last night and the craziest thing happened. The lights of the Capitol and the Washington Monument went off for a few minutes. I thought you should know. Have you heard anything about that?"

Jazzkin was stunned. He wasn't aware the lights had dimmed a second time.

"Erasmus, I saw them dim a couple days ago. I inquired with the Capitol Police, but no one knew anything. This is very strange."

"And you know what's even more strange? I hope you don't mind if I tell you this. We were in Brazil in the rainforest just earlier in the week and my granddaughter had a vision where she saw the lights dim on the Capitol. That's why we returned."

Aria was listening and jumped in the holog, "Hello, Congressman, nice to see you. Let me add I had a vision of some men in dark suits with headphones that had red blinking lights. I don't know what that means."

Jazzkin told them that the music on his speaker also went out when he saw the lights dim the other day. Aria said, "I think we need to bring some healing sounds to the Capitol, Bamps."

"Erasmus," said Jazzkin. "The MUSIC Act is being brought to the House floor tomorrow. I think you should be here. Work with my staff, you can park under the building.

See you tomorrow morning about ten. Thank you. Bye."

They were excited to go to the Capitol the next day, though unsure of what to expect. They thought it would be good to be prepared to share the healing sounds, so Erasmus retrieved a bunch of travel-sized racks, with the pre-tied Live, Fong & Prosper shoestrings. He had several dozen left over from the effort to sell Fonging Kits some years ago. He put them in an old rolling suitcase, with a couple larger racks. He still had a stash of wooden salad forks and spoons, with random other implements and a few turkey basters, and stuffed them in a large backpack. On the way out the door, he also grabbed a special carved walking stick made of hickory, one he felt was quite resonant when hitting the ground.

They piled into the car, with the fonging equipment and a few instruments in case they ended up playing music. They were able to park underneath the Rayburn Building. For a long time after 9/11 and the Insurrection, guests couldn't park there, but things had opened up; the building and garage security cameras could see through cars and identify guns and bombs, like the scanners at the airport.

After arriving and going through security, they took the elevator to the second floor of Rayburn. They were quite the sight, with guitars and fonging equipment. They found Jazz-kin's office, went in, and the friendly staff invited them into a back room, where they waited for the Congressman.

When he arrived, there were introductions all around. Erasmus told him about their trip and explained fonging. The Congressman, being a musician, was very interested in the vibrational qualities. Many think of music as powerful healing sounds of the universe, which is true, of course. The healing sounds of fonging are more primal, and seem able to focus healing intention in particular areas, as they were discovering. Jazzkin really wanted to fong, but was pressed for time and asked Aria more about her vision.

"It was like last night," she told him. "The lights sort of flickered and dimmed and then the lights illuminating the Capitol went out. It was weird having a vision of the men in dark suits with the blinking red lights on their headphones. They seemed involved somehow, but I didn't see them last night."

"But I did feel them," added Neeru.

"I also did notice the tourist people around were very surprised by what they saw, but they didn't make any sound," said Sandro. "It was very peculiar."

"I wonder if this is connected to the MUSIC Act?" asked Aria.

"There are forces that try to divide us, and even prevent us from playing music, because it's so powerful," said Joye. "After what I've seen on this trip, the healing sounds of fonging could be important to counteract the divisive forces."

"You're right, Mizz Joye, I think you're right," agreed Aria.

"Tell you what," suggested Congressman Jazzkin. "Why don't you all watch the proceedings from the upper gallery. If you see the men in dark suits, let me know. I've alerted the police. Now, I've got to get back on the floor."

The Congressman's staff showed them how to get to the House Chamber and to the gallery. They found seats behind the Speaker's rostrum and stuffed their gear and instruments in the row behind them.

"This is amazing, we are here in the United States Congress, seeing democracy at work," said Sandro.

"Just think of how many laws have been debated and passed here," said Joye. "It's easy to criticize Congress, but this institution is key to our freedom. I know it's not perfect, Lordy, but it is impressive."

There was a lot of hubbub on the floor, with Members of the House of Representatives milling around, talking, and gesticulating. A Member would talk for a while, then another one. Congress was about fifty percent women and quite diverse, a thankful change from not too long ago.

"It's like a human rainbow down there," said Joye, nudging Aria's arm as they observed the proceedings. "Thank goodness. I still don't trust the Liberty Party though. They don't seem to want freedom for people like me. I'm glad they're in the minority."

"Jazzkin said this is a really important vote on the MUSIC Act," said Erasmus. "Progressives are in favor of it, but some people just don't seem to understand how powerful and important music is for all of us. It will be interesting to see. Look, there's Jazzkin about to speak."

He pointed down to the floor where Representative Hoyez Jazzkin stood in front of the microphone. The vote was so important that the venerable Speaker Nancee was presiding. She banged the gavel. "The gentleman from Maryland has the floor to introduce the MUSIC Act."

"Ladies and gentlemen of the House," began Jazzkin. "I rise to introduce H.R. 432, Musicians United to Support Instrumental Communities, also known as the MUSIC Act. This legislation is intended to move our society strongly in the direction of a more harmonious union, by supporting musicians who bring us so much joy and happiness. It is also designed to support communities where people can live together and share resources with the common purpose of supporting music and the arts. These communities can lift our spirits and bring us together. It's critical that we search our souls, develop our goals, and create our intentions for a more peaceful and melodious world."

There was applause, but Neeru felt something dissonant. She leaned over to the others and whispered, "I feel that discordant energy again. Keep your eyes and ears open."

Jazzkin continued, "I would like to summarize the key provisions of the MUSIC Act prior to our vote today. The Act will promote more music and support musicians, which will benefit other artists and the public too, by adopting the following key provisions:

Universal Healthcare for musicians, so that they do not have to worry about their health coverage and related financial implications, but can focus on music;

Universal Basic Income for musicians, so that they can count on a certain basic level of income and not have to work menial jobs rather than devoting full time to music;

Stronger Copyright Laws, to protect copyrighted works of musicians that will generate additional income for them;

Music Education, in the schools so that children will reap the benefits of learning music, which helps them in other academic pursuits, as well as music education for adults;

Accessible Music Venues, meaning that appropriate places for musical performances and gigs, house concerts, and the use of church space in particular, will be more available so that musicians don't have to play for pennies in bars;

Restoration of Urban Areas, such as the many small towns that have declined because of large corporations, with the intention that music can once again fill those towns with hope and good vibrations;

Encouragement to have a Song Open all Meetings, in Congress, the Administration, Courts, federal and state governments, as well as administrative bodies, nonprofit organizations, and corporations, so that everyone will be in the most harmonious frame of mind when deliberating and making decisions;

Enforcement of Noise Statutes, to reduce noise pollution, especially in urban areas, which contributes to stress and adversely affects wildlife, including the designation of 'quiet towns' to reduce traffic noise during evening hours; and finally, to

Promote Music Ashrams, as a way for musicians to share resources and provide music and education to the communities for the betterment of all."

"Madam Speaker," called out Jazzkin. "I move the adoption of the MUSIC Act!"

The House erupted in applause, just as the lights started to flicker.

"Oh, no," cried Aria. She looked around, then pointed to the other side of the gallery. "Do those men in the dark suits over there have headphones with blinking lights?"

They turned to look, but the lights continued to flicker and no one could see them clearly. The lights dimmed and then got bright again, over and over, almost like a strobe light. Members of the House began shouting.

Speaker Nancee pounded the large gavel and cried out,

"Order, order in the House!"

All of a sudden, the shouting stopped. Joye said, "But their mouths are still moving! What's going on?"

It was almost comical. Members of the House of Representatives talking and shouting, flailing their arms, but there was no sound.

"I feel that dark energy again; everything is out of phase," whispered Neeru. "We need the healing sounds!"

"It's those guys with the suits and headphones, I know it," proclaimed Aria. "I'm going down there. They need a good fong!" She quickly reached behind her and pulled out one of the larger pre-strung racks from the suitcase. Then, she stood up, balanced on the brass guard rail, and surrendered to her inner space. "I trust you Spirit of Music," she implored. "Please help me again."

With that, she tight-rope danced across the front of the gallery, jumped off the rail, grabbed the ledge under the ornate clock over the rostrum, and swooped down next to the Speaker.

"Hi, Speaker Nancee, mind if I fong?" She sprang onto the Speaker's lectern and stood high over the House floor, where Members continued to soundlessly shout and gesture.

Erasmus saw what she was going to do, but realized there was no implement to tap the rack. He grabbed his hickory walking stick, caught Jazzkin's eye, and flung the stick to him. It sailed through the air and Jazzkin caught it with one hand. He looked at Erasmus, who mouthed the words, "Tap the rack!"

Aria saw what Erasmus had done, and put her fingers in her ears.

Jazzkin realized what he needed to do, and ran to the front of the rostrum where Aria was standing tall on top of the podium. He reached the stick up and began to tap on the rack that Aria held.

Perhaps it was the importance of the moment. Maybe their intention to spread peace. Or the power of trust in one another and in democracy. But whatever it was, Aria felt the healing sounds well up inside her like never before. They were beautiful, powerful, but no one else could hear them. She saw them all looking at her, as the lights dimmed lower, and she knew what she must do.

Aria channeled the fonging experience from Rishikesh, where those all around felt the vibrations. She felt the energy of the plants. She opened her mouth and sang out as loudly and confidently as she ever had. She felt as if she were in a special space, where she was watching the healing sounds flow through her. It was like the Spirit of Music was singing, not her!

"Ahhhhhhhhhhhhhhhhhhhh, eeeeeeeeeeeeeee, aaaaaaaaaaaaaaa!"

"Oh, my," gasped Neeru. "She sang the Faad note!"

The effect was immediate. Everyone in the House chamber froze and stared at Aria. The lights came on brighter than before and a loud cheer went up. "Yaaayyyy!"

"There is sound again!" hollered Sandro. "Yahoo!"

"I don't see those guys in dark suits," said Erasmus, scanning the audience. He thought he saw some very dim red lights, but couldn't be sure.

Aria remained standing on the podium. She took her fingers out of her ears. Then she called out, "Members of

Congress. I've demonstrated for you the power of the healing sounds of the Universe through fonging. We have been travelling around the world for the last month, and I can attest to the beneficial aspects of fonging. We hope that we've helped silence those who would divide us, those who would force us out of phase. We hope you see the power of sound and implore you to pass the MUSIC Act!"

The Members of Congress roared their approval and applauded!

Congressman Jazzkin hollered out, "Reclaiming my time! I offer an amendment to the MUSIC Act. Not only shall we have a song before every session and meeting here in Congress, but I move unanimous approval to amend the Act so that we have both a fong and a song before every meeting!"

Again, the Members of Congress hollered their approval.

Speaker Nancee pounded the gavel. "The amendment is accepted by voice vote. All in favor of passing the MUSIC Act, say Aye!"

"Aye!" responded the Representatives.

"No one can be opposed to that," said Speaker Nancee with a smile. "The MUSIC Act is hereby adopted!"

"We wanna fong! We wanna fong!" The Members began chanting.

"Sandro, let's get these racks and implements out and just toss them down there," called out Erasmus.

They grabbed the small racks and implements and started flinging them out from the upper gallery to the floor of the House. Members caught them in the air or scurried after them, picking them up and trying to figure out how to fong. Erasmus, Sandro, and Neeru raced down the stairs and started giving impromptu fonging lessons. The Representatives were all jumping up and down, hollering, and dancing in celebration.

Joye had remained up in the gallery and pulled out her guitar. She stood up and hollered loudly, "In honor of this historic event, what historians may one day call a Fongsurrection, I have a song for you. The MUSIC Act requires a fong, which you have had, but now we need a song. Here is one of my favorites; Lift Every Voice and Sing, also known as the Black National Anthem. Please sing along with me."

Lift every voice and sing
Till earth and heaven ring
Ring with the harmonies of Liberty
Let our rejoicing rise
High as the listening skies
Let it resound loud as the rolling sea.

Sing a song full of faith that the dark past has taught us
Sing a song full of the hope that the present has brought us
Facing the rising sun of our new day begun
Let us march on till victory is won.

Once again, everyone applauded and cheered. It was a big fong fest down on the House floor. Aria and Erasmus were fonging with Speaker Nancee and Jazzkin in a couples fong.

"This is quite a vibrational endeavor, these sounds," said Speaker Nancee. "I love it."

Erasmus said, "We've been finding that the healing

sounds of fonging infuse positive and beneficial vibrations that can address social problems. I believe they'll help engender trust again in our democracy; it's so critical."

Jazzkin agreed, "Just look at all these Congressman, I've never seen them enjoy one another so much. And thank you Aria for your bravery in jumping up on that podium and fonging; what a voice, it was awesome."

Aria replied, "It was a privilege. I trusted the Spirit of Music and it worked out OK."

"It sure did," said Speaker Nancee. "Thank you all so much."

"Thank you both for everything," said Erasmus. "So glad you're our Congressman, Mr. Jazzkin." He gave Jazzkin an impromptu hug.

"Thank you, Erasmus, and Aria, amazing, and all of you. What can I say? Fong on!" He reciprocated with hugs all around and went back to celebrating with his colleagues.

Just then, Sandro came over and spoke quietly to Erasmus and Aria. "I am feeling some strong rhythms. I don't know where they are coming from. Neeru felt them too. Do you feel these sounds?"

Aria and Erasmus paused and listened with their ears and their souls.

Whoom, swoosh, whoom, swoosh, ahh; whoom, swoosh, whoom, swoosh, ahh ha.

"Yes, goodness, what is that?" asked Erasmus.

"You know," said Sandro. "It reminds me of canoe paddling of indigenous people I have heard in the Amazon."

Neeru joined them. "The sounds are becoming more loud. I sense an intention that the sounds are coming for us.

I am seeing vision of a dock along a river, with a large building looming over. What is Nationals Park?"

Erasmus chimed in, "The Washington Nationals baseball stadium. It's right on the Anacostia River. There's a pier there. It's only a few blocks from here. We can walk."

"Yes," said Neeru. "We must go. I feel we should be there soon."

"OK," said Aria. "Let's get Mizz Joye and our gear and see what's up next!"

CHAPTER SEVEN

AN ISLAND OUT OF TIME

They made their way out of the Capitol through the gift shop towards the south. Walking across the Capitol grounds after the successful Fongsurrection made their steps lighter. That was not only because they'd left almost all the racks and implements behind, but they just felt happy. There'd been an immediate demonstrable response to fonging; the MUSIC Act had passed largely because of their actions. And it seemed like they had stymied those dastardly men with the blinking headphones, at least for the moment.

"That was so much fun, y'all," called out Aria. They hustled past the Rayburn House Office Building on their right, and the Longworth Building on their left. It was now afternoon, and the winter sun was heading lower.

"You're tellin' it, Aria," replied Joye. "What an amazing voice you have!"

"That was all the healing sounds, Mizz Joye. It didn't

seem like I had anything to do with it. And holy smokes, that rendition of the Black National Anthem was incredible! Fong-tastic, for sure!"

Erasmus added, "It's probably the first time that song was ever performed in the United States Capitol, Mizz Joye. Truly historic. I was crying it was so powerful." Erasmus shed a tear as he strode down the street with his walking stick.

"The entire experience was so amazing," said Sandro. "I cannot even believe my own eyes and ears. I like this Washington, DC as you call it! Fongs and songs for democracy!"

Erasmus added, "And I just want to say how proud I am of my purple haired granddaughter. So fongtabulous. Really all of you. That was incredible."

They crossed C Street and waved to the Capitol Police standing guard, who smiled and waved back.

"I hope they don't think we have bear spray or anything," whispered Erasmus. "I'm glad they put those Insurrectionists in prison."

"But Fongsurrectionists like us just want to bring the healing sounds to everyone, right Mizz Joye?" said Aria.

"You're right about that," replied Joye. "By the way, where are we going this time?"

"I'm not sure, Mizz Joye," replied Sandro, as they continued down South Capitol Street toward Nationals Park. "But I am feeling stronger in my body the deep rhythms. Do you sense these vibrations?"

Whoom, swoosh, whoom, swoosh, ahh; whoom, swoosh, whoom, swoosh, ahh ha.

"I sure do, Sandro, and the sounds are intensifying. What's going on?" Joye was looking around to see if anything looked amiss, like those men trying to put things out of phase.

They walked under the freeway, and now could see Nats Park a few blocks away.

"Let's turn left up here and we can walk right up to the Park, then we'll go down by the Salt Line restaurant, and we can look out on the Anacostia River from there." Erasmus was a Nats fan and had been to many ball games, so knew his way around the area.

When they finally got to the pier on the Anacostia, they didn't see many people around. Just a few couples walking on the boardwalk, and some kids and strollers. But the sound was much louder. They just couldn't see anything that might be causing it.

All of a sudden, it looked like a sonic rainbow was approaching up the river. The water began churning and they saw a wake coming toward them, but there was no boat!

The disruption in the water pulled right up to the pier, as if a large sailing vessel was docking. A moment later, a stunning young woman in Native American dress appeared out of nowhere and stood on the pier. She had jet black hair and wore buckskin leggings, a thin white wampum vest, and a multi-colored headdress with a variety of feathers. She bowed to greet them, then beckoned for them to follow.

Our intrepid fongsters had observed quite a lot in the last month, but seeing a native person step out of nothingness had to take the cake.

"She wants us to go with her?" asked Joye incredulously. "Into the water?"

"There is a wooden sailing craft of some kind," said

Neeru. "I just can't see it with my eyes."

The woman waved again for them to follow her, and she stepped off the pier and vanished into the air! They were speechless.

Sandro called out, "The rhythms have stopped. But where did she go?"

"Spirit of Music, please help us once again," implored Aria, shaking her head and looking to the sky. Aria walked to where the woman had been, cocked her head to listen, stepped off the pier with her foot over the water, and disappeared!

"Hey, where are you taking my granddaughter?" hollered Erasmus. He ran to help Aria, and also disappeared over the water.

"Don't leave us here," shouted Sandro. With that, he, Neeru, and Joye followed and - to anyone watching - disappeared, too. Then, the vibrations began again.

Whoom, swoosh, whoom, swoosh, ahh; whoom, swoosh, whoom, swoosh, ahh ha.

The turbulent water headed south toward the confluence of the Anacostia and Potomac Rivers.

* * * * * *

Aria had stepped out over the water, listening deeply to her heart and trusting in the Spirit of Music, which was becoming her constant frame of mind. Her foot hit something solid and, as she took her next step, she saw it. It was a giant dugout canoe. There were a dozen men and women ready at the oars.

The woman who beckoned them extended her hand to help Aria down into the canoe, as she did for Erasmus and the others as they boarded. She pointed to short benches where they could sit.

The canoe was nearly forty feet long and twelve feet wide. It was made of a giant old chestnut tree, once ubiquitous in North America, which had gone virtually extinct because of overlogging and disease from pests.

Now they realized what the sound was as the huge canoe got underway; the oars of the canoe were pulled in intricate time by both the men and women paddlers. They soon reached a really fast cruising speed. It seemed the sequencing of the paddles stabbing into the water amplified their speed.

Whoom, swoosh, whoom, swoosh, ahh; whoom, swoosh, whoom, swoosh, ahh ha.

They settled in and looked around as the canoe moved rapidly through the water into the Potomac. Sandro glanced back and could see the Capitol, the Washington Monument, and the rest of the Washington skyline behind them, basking in the afternoon sunlight. "It is so amazing this viewpoint, a shining city so beautiful and important to the world. And now we are going to visit the ancestors."

They pulled their collars up, as the speed of the canoe in the northwest wind made it chilly. The cold didn't seem to bother these lightly clad people, though. Several of them, including some women, wore no shirts. Their tanned bodies were incredibly strong. They seemed like Native Americans from a long time ago. How was that possible? Who were they?

"My name is Soft Snow. I am with the Great Heron Clan

of the Piscataway tribe of the lower Potomac River. Our Clan Mother sent us for you because your vibration matches with our island. She can explain more when we reach the island."

"Our vibration matches with your island?" thought Aria out loud.

"She must mean the healing vibrations of fonging," said Neeru.

"This sailing vessel itself almost feels like fonging; the vibrations of the paddling are intense," said Erasmus.

"It will be a couple hours of canoeing down the river," said Soft Snow. "We have some water for you here in this clay jug. Please relax and enjoy the ride."

They didn't know where they were going. It seemed they'd been kidnapped by a bunch of Indians! They just watched the banks of the Potomac River pass by as they raced down the river, propelled by the incredible strength of the paddlers, a growing northwest wind behind them, and the full moon tide rushing down toward the Atlantic Ocean.

* * * * * *

The sun was about to set on their right when the Potomac grew much wider. They passed under a tall bridge and by a couple of small islands on the left, one with a large white cross. Not too much later, Joye thought she saw a rainbow. "Look there," she pointed ahead a little to the port side. "It's a double rainbow, but it isn't raining!"

It looked to be a double rainbow, but they would never imagine what it really was. As they came closer, it appeared to be a large dome, lighter on the inside.

"You can only see it because you are in our canoe," explained Soft Snow. "No one else can see it."

"What is that I am feeling?" asked Sandro. "My hairs on my arms are standing up. I feel strong vibrations all around."

"Me, too, my brother," agreed Erasmus. "It seems to be coming from the dome ahead."

"Oh, my," gasped Aria. "That isn't a rainbow of light; it's a dome of sound. It's so huge! And we're going right into it!"

The humongous dugout canoe lurched as it entered through the aural curtain. Loud thunder groaned as if they'd crossed the sound barrier.

"Oh, my," exclaimed Erasmus, as the water smoothed out. "Feel that peace and wholeness. This is unbelievable."

"I think this must be heaven," added Sandro. "Mizz Joye, what does it feel to you?"

"It feels like three shots of my favorite tequila. And motherhood," answered Joye. "I've never felt anything like this."

"It's like we're surrounded by divine feminine energy, completely," said Aria, gazing at the island they could now see, with giant trees and white beaches.

Neeru placed her hand over her heart. "My friends, we are experiencing the essence of the Faad." She turned to Soft Snow and said, "You have tapped into the ultimate reality of sound, the key note of the universe. What do you call it?"

Soft Snow was also staring at the island, her home. "We call it, the Sound of Peace."

The paddlers slowed from their frenetic pace and the canoe glided toward a small cove on the north end of the island. They rounded a rocky spit of sand and then slid in the protected water to the shore. It was dusk, but they could make out a large group of people in Native dress waiting for them.

The canoe came to rest between several timbers standing in the water, to which the paddlers tied stout ropes to secure it from the wind or tide. A wide plank was put in place to walk on to shore. As they disembarked, a young man on shore played a small wooden drum and others shook rattles made from turtle shells decorated with paint and feathers. Another played a flute and a few chanted to welcome their visitors. The other people lightly tapped their cupped hands together in various rhythms consistent with the drumming, as if applauding their guests arrival.

Standing tall in the center of the group were a man and woman, clearly the leaders of the tribe. He stood with a many feathered headdress, wampum belt, and buckskin clothes. She wore a simpler headdress, with many beads around her neck and a long skirt also of buckskin decorated with shells and beads.

"Welcome to Swan Island. I am the Clan Mother, Whispering Wind." She bowed to them.

"And I am Chief Strong Bear. Soft Snow told you we are the Great Heron Clan of the Piscataway tribe. We heard and felt you since the last moon. We have much to share. Please join us for a meal and some rest."

"Thank you so much," said Erasmus with a bow. "We are delighted and amazed to be here. My name is Erasmus. Please meet my granddaughter Aria, and our dear friends Mizz Joye, Neeru, and Sandro. We've been traveling around the world and experienced much together of the strong vibrations like you have here. We thank you for your hospitality and look forward to learning about this wonderous place."

Soft Snow beckoned them follow her up the path. As they shuffled after her, the drumming and shaking continued. Whispering Wind turned and said to Aria, "Thank you for bringing the healing sounds to the world. We are kindred spirits."

"Sure thing! This is all so amazing," agreed Aria.

"I love the color of your hair, Aria," said Whispering Wind.

They walked over a hill and across a small ridge, the trees looming over them. Loblolly pines, oaks, and chestnuts. "These trees are like in the Amazon rainforest," said Sandro. "They are ancient trees that have never been cut it seems to me."

"How's that possible?" asked Erasmus. "We're in the middle of the Potomac River, not too far south of where I live, I'm sure of it. I've never heard of this island."

"We have a lot to learn about this place," said Joye. "It sure does feel peaceful."

"It feels like home to me," added Neeru.

They crested another hill and descended to a large flat village area with eight longhouses, built of bent saplings and covered with tree bark. Each house was about sixty feet long, maybe twenty feet wide, with a curved roof twenty feet high. In the center of the town were raised steps leading to an open plaza. From there, one could look south toward the open expanse of the river toward the Chesapeake Bay. The hill and trees blocked the prevailing winter wind from the northwest, so it was relatively warm in the village.

Soft Snow showed them into one of the houses. A couple fires burned, and the smoke went out covered holes in the roof. Several families lived in each longhouse, so maybe fifty people in each; their belongings and beds were on raised platforms made of branches. A few women and girls were weaving baskets and sewing clothes, while some of the men worked on making tools, their jobs during the winter months. Each visitor was provided a sleeping area. They put down what they had brought with them, which wasn't much, and greeted those who lived there. Soft Snow then took them out to the plaza.

Whispering Wind and Chief Strong Bear called for everyone to assemble, and they all sat down. The Clan Mother spoke first. "We have been fortunate to learn of these modern humans who have come to our island by listening to their vibrations. They have brought their healing sounds to several parts of the earth. They initiate the sounds through an unusual activity; these sounds are of the same key note as our Sound of Peace. We welcome them and look forward to learning more of their beneficial achievements."

The crowd of native peoples again clapped with their cupped hands in approval. The red hue of sunset began to give way to the dark blue night sky. Several stars appeared, as the wind moderated.

Chief Strong Bear next spoke. "We shall share our meal with them tonight and have conversation, for tomorrow night we shall have a celebration!"

There were whoops and more clapping. "But first," said the Chief. "We shall begin with The Words That Come Before All Else to share our gratitude. Soft Snow, will you please recite the words."

"Yes, Chief." She turned to the visitors. "The core of our beliefs is respect, for all things. This is essential. And also sharing, for no one owns anything. We are rooted in a culture of gratitude. This world is a gift. We have known the world in which you live, in which all human life is a market of money. If the world is a market, from one's perspective, one grows poor. When all the world is a gift, we become wealthy beyond measure."

The people were quiet and listening intently to Soft Snow. Their visitors were taken by how a powerful perception of gratitude now pervaded the group.

Soft Snow continued, "We have learned these words from many years ago. They come from the Haudenosaunee; people from outside call them the Iroquois. These words may also be called the Thanksgiving Address, for we begin our ceremonies with these words of gratitude to all of creation. Everyone says the words a little differently."

The drum began to play, and several rattles shook. The top of the moon began to rise over the water in the east, and it would become huge and orange above the horizon before continuing its ride to the stars.

Soft Snow began:

We look around at our family and our new friends. We are grateful for them and for the cycle of life that brings us together. We are grateful for one another, for without all of us, there are none of us. Together, we give thanks for each of us as people of the earth and recognize our common humanity. Now, our minds are one.

The group responded to this by repeating: *Now, our minds are one.*

We give thanks to our mother, the Earth. She provides all

that we need for life and supports all the plants and animals. Everything that we are and have is here, thanks to Mother Earth. We will protect her and keep her safe. We would be nowhere without her and give her our gratitude every day. Now, our minds are one.

We recognize that water is life, and we thank the water of the earth in all its forms; rain, snow, mist, streams, rivers, and oceans. We could not exist without the waters; we drink the water and are made of water. The waters come from the sky and bubble out of the earth for us and all living things. We offer our most sincere gratitude for the waters. Now, our minds are one.

We appreciate the beautiful fish that swim in the waters, and all the animals from the sea, such as, rockfish, sturgeon, crabs, terrapin, and oysters that purify the water. We are thankful that the fish provide us with nourishment so that we can live and enjoy our Mother Earth. Now, our minds are one.

We see all around us the plants, everywhere on earth, small and large. They feed us and all other species. The plants were here first, and we must learn from them to survive on the planet. The plants hold the soil and bring us shade from the sun. The Three Sisters, corn, beans, and squash, nourish us. So many other vegetables, potatoes, berries, and fruits are satisfying nourishment. The medicine plants heal us when we are ill. They talk with us and tell us how they can be used to help us. The trees are wise; they shade us and allow us to construct houses and canoes. They bring us truth and strength. We are so grateful for our plant family. Now, our minds are one.

We see now above the trees, flying in the sky, the birds of many colors, shapes, and sizes. They grace us in their seasons, greet us with their songs, and inspire us with their skills flying in the air. We listen as they serenade us in the morning, and we hear what they tell us. We are grateful for all they teach us in song and life. Birds make us happy, and we thank them. Now, our minds are one.

We appreciate all the animals that walk on and live under the land. We thank them for their beauty and skills, and all they teach us. We are most grateful for those who give up their lives for our nourishment and for all the things we make from them that help us every day. We communicate with and learn from all the animals. We thank them as our brothers and sisters of the land. Now, our minds are one.

We feel the four winds and the cleansing air they provide for us to breathe. They also bring us the seasons that generate so much beauty and newness in our lives. The lightning and thunder remind us of the power of nature and our small role in it, yet they also bring the sustaining water from the sky. Now, our minds are one.

We thank the sun for its light and warmth every day, so that we can see this beautiful earth and so that all life can grow on the planet. We would not be here without the sun, and his brothers the stars in the heavens show us the immense expanse of the universe. We thank also Grandmother Moon, who shines for us at night and regulates the tides of the waters. Grandmother Moon is the leader of all women, and her changing face helps us know the days. Now, our minds are one.

We realize that we do not know everything. So, we thank our enlightened teachers who have come to teach us through the ages. We learn when we listen and pay attention to our teachers, whether they be the shamans, the artists and musicians, or the caring teachers who help us how to live in harmony and to be *at peace. Now, our minds are one.*

Finally, we thank our Creator, that from which all comes, the Sound of Peace. It is this ultimate reality of sound that creates everything, all of us and the plants, animals, stars, rivers, and all that is. The Creator, the unstruck sound, creates all time and space, and all dimensions of this life and any others. We express our deepest gratitude to the Creator for the love that allows us to live in peace and harmony as long as that is our intention. Now, our minds are one.

There was silence. No one said a word for several minutes. For the visitors, they had never experienced gratitude expressed so deeply. They felt as if in a sea of appreciation. They were grateful for the ventures they had experienced in the last month and now for the opportunity to see this amazing island and meet these people. But who were they, and how did they get here? And what was up with the dome over the island that made it invisible?

* * * * * * *

Our plucky fongsters were invited to the longhouse of the Clan Mother for the meal. They were offered an array of venison, fish, oysters, terrapin soup, and an assortment of nuts, berries, and preserved corn, beans, and squash cooked in a stew. The food was presented in clay pottery, decorated with shells and beads. They sat on earthen humps covered with animal skins around the middle fire.

"We thank you for the hospitality," said Erasmus. He began to eat a large oyster, with some sort of indescribable red sauce, but found it too large to slurp, so had to use a sharp bone knife to cut it.

"I'd like to say how moved I was, we all were, with the words spoken by Soft Snow," said Joye. "We could use more of that in our modern society. Gratitude is one thing missing from our world."

They all nodded in agreement as they enjoyed their food, now realizing how hungry they were.

Aria asked, "This is so wonderful, and I have so many questions. First, what creates the dome of sound? Could you tell us about that, please?"

"This story comes from many, many moons ago," began the Chief. "There was a boy of the Great Heron Clan who lived on this island, shortly before the white man Smith sailed up the Bay."

Erasmus interrupted, "You mean Captain John Smith, the Englishman who helped settle Jamestown and wrote his findings about the Bay? The story goes he was saved by the Indian princess Pocahontas."

"Yes, of the Powhatan tribe southwest across the river," replied the Chief. "The white men had just begun to take over our lands. This boy's name was Singing Snakes, for he loved to get in the waters and mud and play with frogs, snakes, and such animals and he always would sing. He had a very resonant voice." The Chief ate a large oyster and continued. "It is told that he was playing by a stream that came out of rocks on the north side of our island. He strung up some oyster shells along braided sweetgrass so that the water would hit the shells. He realized it made a pleasant sound.

So, he used his wits and imagination to construct an array of shells, bound with sweetgrass and strong spider silk, which produced even more harmonious sounds. Soon, there were one hundred shells, tapping upon one another."

Aria asked, "Sort of like a wind chime, but with water?"

"Yes, I think that is a close thing to say," replied the Chief. "And Singing Snakes would construct his water shells and sing the most glorious songs. He did his chores as part of the community to help our people, of course, but they let him spend much time with the shells because the sound was healing for all who listened."

Clan Mother Whispering Wind continued, "Over time, Singing Snakes realized the area around his harmonious construction was very powerful. He felt clear and centered when he was there. Others of the tribe who visited, as the story goes, also felt the power, and began to spend time there. Peculiar things happened. Some objects near the stream would disappear and then reappear again. Wounds seemed to heal faster if one spent time there. Most importantly, the people soon realized their intentions became real very quickly. And all the time, Singing Snakes added more shells, and stronger supports, until there were several hundred oyster shells attached by the sweetgrass and spider silk way up into the surrounding trees. It became a sacred site for us."

"Like a sound temple," offered Neeru.

"Or cathedral," suggested Joye.

"Yes. So, when the white man started coming to our shores and visiting other native peoples," said the Chief, "things began to turn sour. Initially, the people were curious and friendly, but soon ill feelings grew, and we noticed diseases affected the people in many tribes. Our clan called a council and the clan mother at the time, Eagle Eyes, told the people to hold the council at the place Singing Snakes had made. This was very fortunate."

"Indeed," said Whispering Wind. "The council was held to discuss the problems with these new white people. Eagle Eyes represented the feminine energy that wanted peace and to avoid the problems. Many of the warrior men wanted to fight, but Eagle Eyes said to the clan: We must tap into the powerful vibrations from Singing Snakes creation and put forward a strong intention of peace. All were quiet for some time, surrendering to the ultimate force of nature, and manifesting the intention of peace. The elders smoked the traditional pipes with tobacco and sent their intentions to the heavens."

"Wow," said Sandro. "I have felt the strong intentions sent up by the smoking pipes in my country. This is powerful mojo, how you say it?"

"Truth," replied the Chief. "It was potent. Soon a halo began to grow over the area. The people could see it, hear it, and sense it. It was good. They did not understand, but they surrendered to the vibrations, sang and chanted, and the halo grew more and more. Soon, they knew it was coming over the entire island. They did not know how or what it was, but it stayed in place. And somehow, the intention to remain at peace and not be part of the white man's assault became lasting."

Soft Snow said, "Later, the people came to understand that the vibration was from the ultimate life force. They learned that sound creates all things, including time and space. As the intention of the tribe had been to be free from the domination of the invading white man, the pestilence, and the violence, our island became invisible to outsiders. It became of a different time and space. The people of our clan have lived their lives in peace ever since. We learned to go outside and return, and also to let some humans or other species come in when we want. We call Singing Snakes creation, the Sound of Peace Maker."

"Double wow," said Aria. "It's like a time/space warp dome, or something. How amazing."

"Yea, caused by sound," said Erasmus.

"It is the Faad, we call it," said Neeru. "It is so powerful. The Faad is the unstruck sound, the force behind all things."

"And somehow we tapped into it by fonging, if that don't beat all," Joye smiled as she shook her head.

"Soft Snow felt your fonging," said the Chief. "And then Whispering Wind sensed it, too. Soon, we all knew something like our Sound of Peace was out there."

Soft Snow said, "I felt a strange tingle yesterday, and this morning my intuition told me to gather the strongest paddlers of our canoe, go up the river, and find you. I did not know who you were or what was happening, but when we approached to the city you call Washington, I saw your faces in my mind and knew where you would be."

The Clan Mother spoke, "We are grateful that you came to us."

"It was a little dicey, stepping off into an invisible canoe," exclaimed Joye.

The Chief said, "I would suggest that we finish our meal and everyone get some rest. Tomorrow you will visit the place of Singing Snakes!"

* * * * * * *

The next morning, Soft Snow led them on a tour of the
island. The sun rising in the east warmed them in the winter
chill. It was like walking in paradise, with luxurious bushes,
trees, and meadows, and the shining waters of the Bay never
too far in the distance. Before long, they came to a grove of
large trees, mostly loblolly pines, and very tall. They noticed
what looked like a large white ship's sail, but as they got closer, they began to hear it. They soon saw it was an immense
array of oyster shells strung together, maybe fifty feet into the
air, tied up to the trees! It was the Sound of Peace Maker!

"Those are some huge oyster shells," exclaimed Erasmus, leaning on his walking stick. "Much bigger than the
ones we have, uh, in the modern era. Sheesh, these are right
down the river from us. I've heard the oysters were much
larger even 100 years ago, much less 500 years ago!"

"Yes, indeed, Erasmus," said Sandro. "These are ginormous. Each oyster shell is like the size of a plate for dinner."

"Oysters used to grow into large reefs, that were even
dangerous to ships passing by. This is like living in the past.
Are we in the past?" Erasmus asked with a quizzical look on
his face.

"Listen to the sound, it is very much subtle, but so
strong," said Neeru. "I feel the tingle."

"Me, too, Neeru," added Aria. "Let's go closer and look."

As they walked down a hill to the shore, they came across
a stream where the water shot out of the rocks and splashed
directly into a couple large oyster shells tied up into the web
of shells above. Those shells twisted and turned when hit

by the water, and knocked into other oyster shells, and so on. The effect was like a giant wind chime and it looked like a massive wall of shimmering leaves in the wind. It made a very unique sound.

"What was it that holds this thing together, sweet grass and spider silk? Man, look at how strong it is?" observed Joye. "How do you get spider silk like this?"

Soft Snow responded, "Singing Snakes initially wove the sweetgrass; it took him a long time. We now regularly repair any places that become weak. The yellow jumping spider has very strong silk, and it does not use the silk for a web, but to jump and catch its prey. He learned to harvest it from the spiders, which then used the structure for their hunting and to build more strands. He knew how to communicate with the spiders and it was a cooperative venture."

"I know that spider silk in the Amazon is very strong, and elastical, too, stronger than steel on the size scale," said Sandro.

Aria asked, "Singing Snakes could talk with spiders?"

Soft Snow laughed, "Yes. We understand the plants and animals. It is more of a deep knowing than talking. Those three deer over there are curious about you who are new to the island. Come say hello."

A doe and two younger deer were watching them from the trees. They looked at the group of strange humans and the doe walked over and sniffed. She looked right at Aria.

"Oh, my life," Aria exclaimed. "The deer is thinking she likes my purple hair!"

Everyone laughed. The deer shook her head, as if to say, of course that's what I was thinking, and the three darted off.

"Oh, look at that spider!" called Aria. She pointed to a bright yellow spider on the tree above. Suddenly, the spider jumped in the air and landed on the strands holding up the oyster array. "That was a long jump!"

About twenty more spiders then made similar long jumps onto the strands and began tending to them. "Wow, those little rascals are working on the strands holding up the Peace Maker," said Joye.

"Yes," said Soft Snow. "They have become its guardians. They repair strands and keep them strong around the sweetgrass. We help sometimes too, but the yellow jumping spiders are very good at their work. We also leave untouched an area of the forest where these spiders live. We are grateful for their help."

They continued their tour around the island, walking under towering trees and down to sandy beaches. They saw many ducks, geese, and swan. They walked by fields where, during the growing seasons, the Three Sisters grew, along with tobacco, strawberries, and other vegetables.

When they returned to the village, the people were intent on their daily tasks. They didn't have any grocery stores or online ordering facility, and had to make everything themselves; clothing, weapons, utensils, you name it. There was a growing sense of anticipation for the big ceremony tonight. It seemed like a good time to relax and play some music, so the fongsters jammed for a while, showing the people their instruments, and learning about the native instruments, including the water drum, shakers, and flute.

* * * * * * *

The festivities began in late afternoon. It was to be a full moon, so there would be light when it rose after sunset. The sky was clear from the northwest wind. Everyone congregated on the plaza around several fires. Several of the people began playing music.

The Chief began, "We are grateful for today. We are grateful for our friends who have visited us. We treasure our relationship with the Sound of Peace, and we want to bring more of these sounds to the world. I believe our friends can help with that."

Erasmus called out, "Yes, Chief, we will do what we can to help the Clan to spread the healing sounds."

The Chief continued, "Thank you, brother Erasmus. We have perceived from our deep listening and intuition something of this fonging activity. I will attempt to describe it to the Clan. Our guests may correct me if I am not accurate."

"So," said the Chief. "Our friends learned of this fonging in some mysterious way, we do not know."

"An angel told us in a dream," chimed in Aria. "First, she came to my grandfather, and then just one month ago, to me. She was a funny angel, and she turned my hair purple, too."

"Ah," replied the Chief. "The gift of fonging came from the spirits; they can be playful sometimes."

Aria nodded and the Chief continued. "To fong, one takes a hard piece of thin pottery in crosshatch. To this they tie sinew, one for each hand to hold; the sinew is wrapped around the main finger of each hand. Now, gather this; the person who is going to hear the fong sounds puts their fingers in their ears."

Many of the villagers started laughing when they heard this. They hooted even more as the Chief continued.

"Then, other humans knock against the rack with some hard bone or wooden stake, like a short spear. It makes the Sound of Peace in the hearing area of the head. It sounds like this."

He didn't make any noise, but seemed to release a virtual sound they could hear. The people began to ooh and aah at the wonderous tones. And laughing some more. And cup clapping, then shouting and hollering!

"You can tell they're hearing the healing vibrations, even though there are no struck notes," whispered Erasmus.

Neeru and Joye piped up at the same time, "I'm hearing them too!"

"Me, too," said Aria. "He is creating the sounds with his aura, or maybe tapping directly into the healing sounds and just sharing them. This is so amazing."

"Oh, I hear it too," said Erasmus.

The Chief then told them, "Here is part of my aural vision I do not understand. Everyone who fongs loves the special sound of an implement I cannot describe. I can best say, it is like a small empty turtle shell affixed to a stick. Hear this."

With that, they all heard with their mind's ear the sound of a turkey baster hitting a rack, but it sounded even better. Everyone started laughing at this and they all began guffawing and slapping one another. When hearing and seeing all this, the visitors also started chuckling and giggling, and everyone soon was laughing and cup clapping like crazy! They had all experienced the healing sounds without any racks being tapped. Literally, the unstruck fonging sound!

"Our visitors have done much good by bringing the Sound of Peace to others around the world. We are so happy to know them and to hear them. I wanted you all to experience what they have been doing so you will understand them and their journey. Was that a good explanation, our new friends?"

Erasmus responded, "Most excellent, Chief. We are amazed by the power of these sounds you have on the island, and very grateful that you found us and brought us here. Thank you."

"Great, then let us now have the pipe of peace to signify harmony among us and to send our intentions to the heavens," said the Chief.

The Chief brought out a beaver skin pouch and extracted two parts: a long wooden pipe stem and a separate stone bowl. "There are important aspects of the pipe, which some call the peace pipe, or sacred pipe," said the Chief. "First, we smoke tobacco, which is sacred for us. We use tobacco as a gift to the spirits. We also present tobacco to Mother Earth when we use some of her bounty, such as when we cut down a tree or harvest fruit. We always ask for permission for what we take from nature."

"We believe life is a gift," said Clan Mother. "It is a gift to walk on the earth, and to be able to eat food, and watch the birds fly. Each of us is a gift, a unique blessing to the world. When you view everything as a gift, then suddenly, you are awash in gifts."

"Yes, I view each person, each animal, plant, and each insect, as a beautiful note, a wonderful part of the harmony of nature," said Neeru. "Right now, I am perceiving with many senses the wonderful love of everyone and everything here now." It was clear Neeru was in tune with this perspective on life.

Clan Mother continued, "Yet with each gift is also responsibility. We believe you should only take what you need and use what you take from nature. And you can't take something without giving back. Humans have an immense capacity for gratitude, and it is a shame for all not to have gratitude at the center of our lives."

"You're telling me, sister," said Joye. "Everything nowadays where we come from is me, me, me. Profit, profit, profit. I don't hear modern folks asking what we can give. That Bozos guy is a perfect example of a taker. Where has that mentality led us? Practically to the destruction of the planet. I like the idea of looking at life as full of gifts, and responsibility."

The Chief reverently took the long stem and placed it into the opening of the bowl. "The pipe is very symbolic for us. The stem represents the male, but the most important element of the pipe is the bowl, which signifies the female aspects of the world. When we join them together, it represents union and balance. It is necessary for there to be balance between the feminine and masculine for a peaceful society."

He placed tobacco into the bowl of the pipe and bowed to each of the four directions of the wind. This act is in supplication to the spirits to hear the intentions and prayers of the people. The native people consider the pipe ceremony a sacred moment in time. One traditionally holds the bowl with the left hand and the stem with the right. When a person takes a puff of the pipe (no inhaling!), they blow the smoke toward the heavens with the hope that the intentions will be fulfilled.

The Chief lit the pipe from a twig in the fire. He then placed the pipe to his lips, closed his eyes, visualized his intentions, took a draw from the pipe, and blew the smoke to the sky. "I ask the spirits for the harmony of the Sound of Peace to touch the world." He then passed the pipe to the Clan Mother.

She repeated the process, blew the smoke to the heavens, and said, "I ask the spirits to lift the veil of fear from the eyes of the humans in the world outside, so they can see our oneness and our sacred and divine aspects." She handed the pipe to Soft Snow, who also drew in the smoke and blew it out, saying, "I thank the spirits for our new friends, and ask that they also smoke of the pipe and send their intentions upward to the spirits."

This was something new for our valiant fongsters. Soft Snow handed the pipe to Neeru on her left, clockwise, as the sun travels the sky. Neeru was hesitant, but took the pipe, drew in the tobacco smoke, and very deliberately blew it to each direction. She paused, then said, "I am thankful for this journey with you all. I am looking forward to returning to India. My intention is that the healing vibrations may help ease the divisions caused by religion in our country, the caste system, in particular. I believe this will come so."

The pipe needed to be replenished, so the Chief filled the bowl. Soft Snow asked Neeru, "What is a caste system?"

Neeru replied, "When some people believe they are better than others, and do not want to give up their social and economic status. It has created a situation where some people in the lower caste do not have equal rights and are looked down upon, generation after generation."

Joye said, "We have that in our country, the United States, but it's the privileged white people at the top and the people of color, including black folks like me and Native Americans, at the bottom."

Soft Snow shook her head. "What a sad concept. Under the Great Law of Peace, the value of everyone, and everything, is the same. We all have different roles and responsibilities, and different passions. But everyone has the same rights to live in peace and to be happy."

Aria exclaimed, "You know of the Great Law of Peace?"

Clan Mother responded, "Yes, it was a well-known development to the tribes almost one thousand years ago. Though we are not Haudenosaunee, tribes throughout the land understood the need for peace. The Great Law of Peace was an oral tradition recounted in wampum brought to us by troubadours, traveling musicians. Our people adopted it in most part as a guide for living together with the people. The Great Law lays out a process for governing, but it is mainly about respect for one another and Mother Earth, being good people, and maintaining peace through thoughtfulness and compassion. We realize we are one, and we do not mind doing what we must for the sake of the tribe."

Aria said, "I've been studying about the Great Law in school. It makes so much sense. It's based on a matriarchal system, which I think is really important and better than the violent patriarchal world we live in."

The Chief filled the pipe and offered it to Joye. "Sure, give me a hit of that, thank you, Chief. I've got some strong intentions I'd love to lift to the heavens."

Joye reverently held the pipe and closed her eyes. She

took a puff and blew the smoke upward. "I ask the spirits
to help people understand how critical social and economic
justice is in our society. Please open their eyes to the plight
of the underprivileged. More importantly, please spirits, help
people see that all of us humans are the same, deserving of
justice, freedom, and liberty. Too many people in our world
are so afraid of being equal that they turn to hate and violence. Please help us with that, yea."

There was silence for a moment as everyone thought on
Joye's message.

"Rock on, Mizz Joye, rock on," said Aria.

Joye handed the pipe to Sandro, who held it for a moment
with his eyes closed. "I say hello to the spirits and ask them to
help humans understand better how to live on the earth. My
heart is hurting for the rainforests and the people in the Amazon. Open the eyes of the people to see the destruction; open
the ears of the people to hear these healing sounds; open our
minds to know the oneness. Thank you, spirits."

The gentle music continued as the pipe came to Erasmus. He bowed his head. "I blow the smoke representing my
intentions to the spirit of the northwest wind, which always
brings clarity to the skies and to our hearts. I ask for this clarity also in human understanding of the importance of good
governance. I am buoyed by the knowledge that the native
peoples developed the Great Law of Peace so long ago, and
hope that the healing sounds will help all of us learn to live in
harmony."

The pipe now came to Aria. She was overcome for a moment by the realization of what they'd all experienced. She
didn't know what to say, so listened with her whole being.

Tears formed in the corners of her eyes. She smiled, then lifted the pipe toward the sky, drew in the tobacco smoke and expelled it into the air with a long, slow exhale.

"I ask the spirits to strengthen the divine feminine in the hearts of all people. As the Chief said, balance of the masculine and feminine is critical for peace. The male energy has been too strong for a long time. I ask that the time for domination and cruelty be over. I ask the spirits to play the song of maternal love loudly, so that men will be filled with reverence and gratitude for the divine feminine and honor women. Thank you."

They were silent, all together in their thoughts. Finally, Clan Mother said, "Aria, I am confused by your request. Do you mean that men in your world do not honor women?"

"Oh, it's so complicated, Clan Mother. Yes, in a way, but no, they don't. In our world, almost all women must be afraid of men, who assault, beat, rape, and murder women all too often."

There were audible gasps from Clan Mother and Soft Snow. "What?" asked Soft Snow. "How could this be? In our society, a man would not think of harming a woman, ever. If he did something like that, he would be punished or ostracized. What is wrong?"

Aria hung her head. It was difficult to acknowledge this disease in their society. "You know, I think about this a lot. I've studied it. My conclusion is that, men are afraid of women, of the power of creation that the women hold. Why would anyone try to keep another person down if they weren't afraid of them?"

Clan Mother reflected on this. It was almost impossible

for her to understand. She knew of the awful fighting and bloodshed before the Great Law of Peace. She had heard of the cruelty of the colonists, the slaveowners, and the terrible armies of modern war. Was it a result of domination by men?

"Aria, you have given me pause. Let me respond. In our society, the women create life; they are the beginning. There is no need for any domination. Women are responsible for bringing up the children to be men and women of sound mind. We look at life as sacred, divine. The men respect us, and know we have their best interests at heart. We seek consensus and harmony through our councils. The men are strong, they build the fires and the canoes. They are the chiefs, but the women select the chiefs. If there were a need for war, the men would not go unless the women agreed it was essential."

They were all listening intently. Joye spoke up, "You're making perfect sense, Clan Mother. So, the women are in charge?"

Soft Snow responded, "No, there is balance. There is no need to dominate or be in control."

Aria said, "That's true from my understanding. Matri-archal societies are not about control. They are egalitarian. They are based on the female line. Mother, how are your families organized?"

Clan Mother spoke, "The people of each longhouse are family of the elder female. Whether other women, or sisters, have children, they are all considered mothers. The men marry and live with the family of the wife. We also have visiting marriages, for many prefer different lifestyles as to sexuality. That is not important to us, because kinship is determined by the mother. But the women are in charge of nourishing the family and run the household."

Erasmus piped in. "This is so interesting. Come to think of it, our society is not like this. Men have been in control for a long time, and have been subjugating women, to the point they were property, not able to vote or have a voice, for hundreds, maybe thousands of years. And now I realize how destructive it has been. Sheesh, you hear about men killing their spouses and girlfriends, harassment in the office, the schools, the military."

"Bamps, for sure," replied Aria. "The western religions are totally patriarchal, the governments are patriarchal, so dominance and oppression become the norm." She paused. This was a hot topic for her since she had chosen to get her masters in matriarchal studies. "You know, there's one sacred right that all women have, or should have. Choice. Women get to choose whether or when to have sex, with who, and even whether to give birth, to have children. You can't take that choice away. Nope."

"The tribes of the Amazon also have reverence for the women," said Sandro. "This is very important to peaceful society. Life is sacred, and so all things, the household chores, the cooking, the planting, they are all sacred. It is better for the men this way, too."

The Chief interjected, "It is heartwarming that we can have these discussions. The Sound of Peace brings about truth and openness. I am hopeful that all you have learned on your travels, you can bring back to your world with the healing sounds. We have now all smoked of the pipe. I shall put it away and thank the pipe and the tobacco for this communal raising of intentions and wholesome conversation." The Chief gently separated the stem from the bowl, cleaned them, and put them back in the pouch.

Aria asked, "So, are there other places like this island that have the dome of time and space and the Sounds of Peace."

Clan Mother laughed. "Yes, we are sure there are."

"Oh, my," gasped Neeru. "The Rishis in India have one, do they?"

"Yes, they do. We have had some interaction with them on a spiritual level. More of a knowing, if you will."

"That makes so much sense. All my life, my long life, I have felt the Rishis were still here." Neeru was smiling. "Thank you. I will try to connect with them when I return home."

Sandro asked, "Are there any other places with the Sound of Peace?"

'Well," said the Chief. "We are not sure. However, we have felt aural symbiosis with another island, a larger island in the vast ocean to the west."

Erasmus guessed, "You mean the Pacific Ocean, on the other side of the American continent?"

"That may be," said the Chief.

"Wow, wonder if it's Hawaii?" responded Erasmus.

"Are there several islands? I have a word come to my mind, aloha," said the Chief.

"Oh, my, yes, Chief, that's Hawaii!" cried out Erasmus. "There are eight islands, it's a magical place."

"Hmm, maybe another one. I feel nine islands," replied the Chief. He scrunched up his forehead and seemed to be counting island images in his imagination.

"Well, I'll be," laughed Joye. "There may be another Hawaiian island that's invisible. Bet that's a special place."

"No kidding," said Aria. "I just love the aloha spirit."

"What means aloha?" asked the Chief.

"Aloha means living in harmony with the people and land, with love, grace, and kindness," said Aria.

"That is the spirit we have here on Swan Island," said Soft Snow.

"You know," said Erasmus, "There's an ancient spiritual practice from Hawaii, it's called ..."

Aria and Erasmus called out at the same time, "Ho'oponopono!" They both giggled.

"Jinx," cried Aria.

"Owe me a coke!" replied Erasmus with a laugh. "It's so amazing, I just remembered. When we were in the rainforest experiencing the plant medicine, a song came to me from the words of Ho'oponopono. Those words are: I love you. I'm sorry. Please forgive me. Thank you."

"What is Ho'oponopono?" asked Clan Mother.

"Well," replied Erasmus. "In Ho'oponopono, they would ask: Did you ever notice that, when you have a problem, you're there? It's a perspective that says, I am responsible for my situation, for my reaction to a situation. The focus is on love, gratitude, and forgiveness. But not just for me, or one person. So, when I say, I'm sorry, I mean, if anyone in my family or if any of my ancestors have caused you harm or distress, I'm sorry; I offer my apologies. And if that is so, please forgive me, forgive us, on behalf of your family and your ancestors."

Aria added, "It may seem crazy, but it tells me I can solve any problem. I can be the cause of peace, I can bring love to any situation, or to the world."

Sandro agreed, "Yes, we have the power to bring the love and make a better world."

"It's such a wonderful practice, to use the words as a mantra," Erasmus continued. "But I always thought gratitude should be emphasized more, and in the song as I heard it, more words came."

Erasmus stood up and began snapping his fingers, and immediately the young man with the drum played along, and the rattles began, too. "Let's give this a go. I will dedicate this song of Ho'oponopono to the women of the world. I am sorry for any hurt or offenses by me, or by any men, ever. Please forgive us. Thank you. We love you." He began singing:

We love you.
We're sorry.
Please forgive us.
Thank you.

We're grateful,
For you.
We appreciate,
And adore you.

Aria joined in, then all the others, and they sang it several times.

Aria called out, "Hey, back atcha, Bamps. And all you men! We love you!"

And a white swan flew across the full moon, rising over the water like a giant orange ball of sound.

CHAPTER EIGHT

WHAT WAS THAT ABOUT?

After a scrumptious organic dinner, everyone was relaxing and enjoying the evening. Our intrepid fongsters found a nice perch on a hill overlooking the Bay, and were sitting around sipping some warm drinks. The water lapped at the shore and the wind had died down.

"Wow, what was that all about?" asked Aria.

"Good question, my purple hair friend," replied Joye. "I never could have imagined all this traveling and fonging around the world when I saw you that first time in New York. And we fonged with Alexander Bozos, I still can't believe it."

"Oh, Mizz Joye," replied Aria. "What a wonderful, strange trip it's been. It's meant so much to travel and unleash the fonging sounds with you. You're the best!" Aria reached over and squeezed Joye's hand. They smiled at one another.

Erasmus added, "I agree! My heart is humming with the healing sounds, with love for you all, and everyone." He paused, took in the peaceful scene, and exhaled. "You know, many years ago, I invited the Spirit of Music into my soul. I said, I'm here for you, whatever you want me to do. It's made my life so much richer. I do have my own goals, you know, peace of mind for myself and peace for the world, and music seems to ease the path to reaching them. But, I swear, nothing prepared me for fonging. It seems to me that music and fonging are similar, in terms of being powerful healing sounds. Are they the same? Where do some vibrations begin, and others end?"

"Well," said Joye. "The most powerful healing sounds for me have been the blues. It's deep music from the heart and the soul. I've lived the blues, for sure; so many of us have lived the blues. But you know what, blues music makes you feel good!"

They laughed at that; of course, any sort of music can make you feel better. As they looked out over the immense expanse of water, they reflected on what had happened, blown away by the experiences they'd had together. They were just breathing in the now.

"I believe you are right, Erasmus, my brother," said Sandro. "The vibrations of fonging are like music. What is the difference, I do not know. Both can heal you of pain and help you let go of fear. That I feel is so important."

"What I notice," said Neeru, "In music, you play an instrument and everyone hears it. With fonging, no one hears what is going in the ears, into the head and soul. The rack and the implements of the tapping are the instruments, but you don't really hear them. Maybe each person is really the instrument?" Neeru laughed. "I do feel that fonging gives a better understanding of the underlying reality of sound, the Faad."

"Oh, you're so right, Neeru," exclaimed Aria. "Fonging has shown me a new world. It gets right to the essence of reality!"

Sandro said, "Yes, and maybe physical reality is just as if an illusion, created by sound. Does that mean if we tap into these sounds, in any form whether music, singing, or fonging, that we also can affect physical reality?"

"Or change the past, or even the future?" asked Joye.

"It seems the Great Heron Clan somehow uses sound to alter time and space, is that changing the past and future?" suggested Erasmus.

"I am thinking they used intention to do that, too," said Neeru.

"In the same way quantum science tells us the observer creates reality," Aria suggested, "Maybe the listener is like an observer? All of us are simultaneously observing and also observed, listening and creating vibrations, collectively. So, what reality do we want to create now?" asked Aria.

Good question to ask, at any time.

"Well," said Joye. "I haven't been home in a month. Maybe just going home is what I want to do. I'm going to re-dedicate myself to social and economic justice. If fonging can change that Bozos guy, then anything is possible, and I'm here to do whatever I can. I know we can make our economic system more beneficial for everyone, it just takes perseverance. Although, I have to say, we could also go try to find that invisible Hawaiian island, that would be fun!"

"Oh, that would be fabulous, Mizz Joye," agreed Neeru.

"I think next I want to return to India and me and Raj, we will look for the Rishis. Maybe they can tell us how they made that box with the fonging implements! And I want to focus on trying to take some of the fear out of religion and the caste system with the help of the healing sounds, and music. That would be very good for my country."

Sandro chimed in, "I am going back home and continuing my path of helping seekers find spiritual growth. That is my calling. And I will also devote lots of energy to helping the rainforest. The healing sounds have made a difference, but we need more people to understand the peril of the plants and animals of the Amazon. And I hope you all will come again to visit!"

"Tell you what," said Erasmus. "I want to get back home and do what I can to protect democracy. I think democracy needs music, and music needs democracy, too! I'd like to organize some concerts for democracy. Musicians are very powerful and if they have the intention of supporting freedom and equality, I think it can make a big difference. But I also want to travel to other countries and see if we can set up more music ashrams. How about Australia? We can visit the Aboriginal people. And Africa? Who wants to go? We'll just travel around, playing music, and fonging with people wherever we can, how about that?"

"Oh, Bamps, that sounds like a great plan!" agreed Aria. "For me, I want to go home. I need to finish my masters degree. One of the most important things I think I can do - in addition to spreading the healing sounds - is to focus on uplifting women in our society."

Aria stood up and began walking around, moving her

hands in the air, and getting excited about the topic. "We've gotten way out of balance; the patriarchy is too strong, violent, and oppressive. I think we've lost our connection with nature, with Mother Earth. I know I spoke with her during my experience with the plant medicines. If we listen to her more, and embrace the divine feminine, we can have a more peaceful society, I'm sure of it!"

Excellent point!

"Thank you," said Aria. "It's like we can be more in tune with the morphic resonance of the sonic cosmos, and harmonize better together in our lives. I think we're coming into a new age of musical and artistic expression around the planet. I just love the gratitude and gift economy principles they have here on the island, that so many indigenous peoples had. It seems so much more beneficial for everyone. Working on eliminating fear of one another and promoting peace and harmony. Yea, that's what I want to do."

"Well done, Aria!"

Who was that? Was that the angel's voice?

"It certainly is! You all have accomplished so much through fonging, I am so proud." The angel didn't seem to be physically present, but they could all hear her.

"Hi there, angel," called out Erasmus. "So happy you came to visit my amazing granddaughter, and look what she's been able to do in just a month! She pulled us all together somehow to bring the healing sounds to all these places around the world."

"Aw, shucks, Bamps," said Aria.

"I know, she has done so well. I am very proud. Rekindling the spirit of fonging is so important. In a sense, everyone can do that, but there's more to do, you know," said the angel.

"I was afraid of that," said Joye.

The angel continued, "You have all made good suggestions for next steps. Please do plan to get together again. If you listen, if you feel and are open to the vibrations, you will know when the time is right and where to go. Others will join in your effort. This is an inflection point in history. You have Mother Earth and the Spirit of Music on your side, and you have one another. There will be times that may not be easy, but you have shown determination, resilience, and trust in the healing sounds. Be not afraid. We are very pleased with you all. Fong on!"

They heard the wisps of her wings as she left. Quite a nice angel, do you wonder who or what sent her?

"I sure do," said Aria. "Wait, who said that?"

Ah, I am the unstruck sound. I am the Faad.

"What?" asked Aria. "I think you're the narrator!"

Why can't I be both?

They all sat silent, dumbfounded. Let me explain. The Faad, the ultimate reality of sound is and creates a holographic universe of vibration, which echoes through all of existence. I am, and we all are, simply cosmic vibrations organized into form.

"That's trippy," said Aria.

"It makes sense to me," said Erasmus. "What else?"

Each vibration, of fonging or of music, or of anything, holds within it every other vibration in the cosmos; all vibrations that ever were, and each vibration yet to be.

"Like overtones?" asked Aria.

Yes, exactly! The Faad is just one vibration, and leads to every other vibration in the universe. And the vibrations are holographic, and are the basis of all energy and matter, everything!

"We have tapped into something very deep," said Neeru.

"I think I want to write a book and have this narrator in my book. That would be super cool," said Sandro.

It will be, of course.

"I've got a question," said Joye. "What if there's no vibration, like in space or somewhere."

It's important to recognize that the absence of vibration is equivalent to non-existence.

"Whoa," exclaimed Erasmus. "I'm glad I'm vibrating."

And, get this, the contemplation of non-existence is the origin of compassion.

"That's so interesting," said Aria. "I'm so happy we could all be together for this adventure. And let's do this again soon!"

You have been such wonderful characters. And what a great story! Best Fongsurrection ever! The MUSIC Act in the United States; how about in all nations? And just loving this island out of time and space. We will continue. We will be together again, yes, we will. I will just leave you with this final vibration.

<FONG ON>

LOOKING BACK AND MOVING FORWARD

BY ROY 'FUTUREMAN' WOOTEN

Fonging is an unusual word, and this book *Fonging for The World* by Jefferson Glassie presents a charming and unusual story that takes a deep dive into a new sound experience and the Spirit of Music.

There is the Dogon tribe of ancient priests from Mali who teach that Music is a conscious force that has existed before the beginning of the world. They also revealed to French explorers the mysteries of Sirius A and the unknown Sirius B stars before science knew of or had telescopes to prove the correctness of their knowing.

It is in honor of this kind of transcendent understanding and discovery that I write about *Fonging for The World*. The word fong rhymes with song, and both words (fong and song) resonate like the vibrational spokes of a cymatics wheel of music.

In this story, the healing sounds of the universe of fonging lead us to a new kind of song or sound vibration inspiring
humans, animals, plants, and inanimate objects to not drift
into stagnant cesspools of putrid disharmony and disorder,
but to dance with a fluid reality alive inside every cell.

I first met Jefferson Glassie at my brother Victor Wooten's Spirit of Music camps and I love how Jefferson is
manifesting his dreams and visions with the projects that he
shared with me during our many conversations. His story
presents a unique vision about the Spirit and value of Music
and, with this ideal, Jefferson has created a fantastic and
charming tale.

Fonging for the World presents Music as a central protago-
nist and vibration as a central theme, which brings together
a group of separate personalities to meet a world uniquely
ready for these healing sounds. With an intrepid band of exotic personalities, unlikely musicians, and unusual sounds, the
discoveries made through fonging weave a tale vast enough
to soothe a troubled world and bright enough to shine on the
mystery of the unknown and the unseen.

The power of Music has always provided a way to bring
audiences to a new state of awareness and inspiration. From
church rituals to political rallies, Music has always sup-
plied a centralizing force that unites both the mind and the
heart. Music inspires the intellect and the emotions to move
inward, outward, and Onward.

There are examples shown in a documentary called *Alive
Inside*, where playing favorite music to an individual con-
sistently brings them back from stagnation to fluidity and
life, from an elderly state of isolation and dementia to a fully

engaged personality, from sitting in a wheelchair to standing up and dancing again!

Fonging for the World takes us through a transformational journey with Music and vibration that connects deep into our bones, our inner ear, and our unknown senses. This sonic tale shows how sound and vibration can help bring a world from a state of perpetual sluggishness to a state of fluidity, dancing and moving Onward again!

My journey to present commentary to this story started with a challenge to not simply write a foreword or review a beautifully conceived and wonderful tale, but to look at the story from a backwards and forwards, and ultimately Onward, perspective -- where the audience is encouraged and left to individually ponder and consider, what just happened, what do we want now, what do we choose now, what do we create now, and where do we go next?

I believe this is a good challenge for all groups, from business owners to essential workers, from politicians to political parties, from the right side of the fence to the left side of the brain, to look within existing ideals, perspectives, and ideological differences and find the way to move away from water slowly dying in a cesspool of deadly sameness to water that is alive inside, flowing forward, and Onward with the Spirit of Music .

Music allows the variation of the sound of instruments to be different and not default to atonal disharmonious conflict, but to make a symphony of life through the creative use of those differences. Using sound as an idea, the central characters of this book are each whisked away from their familiar worlds (like in the Wizard of Oz) to join forces like separate drops creating a deep ocean of inspiration beyond normal daily life and politics as usual. These unlikely heroes learn the spiritual dimensions of Fonging, Music, and vibration as a pathway to create fluidity and movement flowing with harmony enough to refresh global inertia.

Thank you Jefferson Glassie for sharing your story with us. With this Onward movement, I give a toast to you and all of your listeners and readers to fong on to the vibration, the Music and the dance that speaks directly to your mind, your body, your heart, and your inner ear.

Fong On!

GRATITUDE

BY JEFFERSON GLASSIE

ey, Namaste, thank you so much for reading and/
or listening to Fonging for the World. I hope you've
enjoyed the story and maybe even learned a little
something, too. I have many people to thank who
contributed to this effort, but first let me say this:

If there's anything you want to do to make this world
more loving, peaceful, and harmonious, no matter how crazy
it might seem, give it a shot. I mean, this fonging thing is
nutty, preposterous, and inane, but to the extent we can learn
about and spread an understanding of the healing sounds
of the universe, I decided to just put it out there. Why not? I
believe fonging will be helpful and nurturing to the cause of
peace, and it's a lot more sane than war! So, set your intention to reach the highest and best goal you can, and just go
for it, no matter what anyone says or thinks. And if you ever
thought about writing a book, consider producing an audiobook too. Trust in the Spirit of Music, and Fong On!

I am profoundly grateful for the opportunity to write

this book and produce two audiobooks, and I have so many people to thank. First, for inspiration, mentorship, and showing me more than I can explain, I want to thank Victor Wooten. His two books and audiobooks – *The Music Lesson* and *The Spirit of Music* - enthused me in so many ways. First, the idea that you can make an audiobook that's a soundtrack for a book is fongtastic! I wrote this book basically so I could create an audiobook. Vic showed me how to do it; model the characters on people you know and ask them to read their parts. The process was incredibly rewarding for me, and I hope for everyone who participated. I'm also very hopeful it will help motivate other musicians and artists to do the same. I also want to thank Vic for opening so many doors to incredible thinkers and musicians, and for introducing me to the entire Wooten Woods community, especially the Spirit of Music campers.

The audiobooks would not have been possible without Dave Welsch. He helped Vic with his audiobooks, so he was the go-to producer for me. We had almost twenty characters, six songs, and all sorts of random sounds, including oven racks and turkey basters, and he put it all together. Dave is remarkable, and also does film scores, you know, if you have any audiobooks or movies you need produced.

I basically let the Spirit of Music guide me through this process and early on I heard Michael Kott's voice as the narrator. He was the inspiration for the teacher Michael in Vic's books, and is a musical shaman and one of the smartest people I know. My podcast interview with Michael in 2018 changed the whole enchilada for me and his voice was perfect as the narrator. I am grateful for Michael's wisdom.

My first granddaughter Mae is such a joy for me, and now there is Rosemary, too! My hope for humanity and our planet is deeply embodied in these two wonderful creative forces. It wasn't easy anticipating what they might be like when older, but I just trusted as I was writing. Kathleen Hooper is a marvelous singer, and I had taken voice exploration sessions with her at the suggestion of my son Max. Synchronicity brought us together when she was in Peru and I asked her to play this role. She is delightful, kind, generous, and the perfect singer and spirit for the character of Aria.

One of my real sheroes in life is Gaye Adegbalola, fabulous musician and powerful griot. I have admired her for years; she inspires me with her courage and she was totally supportive and down with this project from the git-go. I could not be more thankful for her participation, in particular, the two amazing songs she did for the audiobook. And it was such a treat for her Queen Lovelace to read the part of the Angel; it was perfect!

In February of 2020, I had the good fortune to have a meeting in Delhi, India and then somehow was led to the Devi Music Ashram in Rishikesh. It literally changed my life, and my relationship with the wonderful musicians at the Ashram has also been transformative. I so much appreciate Devi Kumar who played Neeru and Raj Sagonakha, who read his part and consulted with me on many of the conversations about India we had in the book. I truly believe the world would be a better place with more music ashrams, which is why we formed the International Music Ashram Association. Every home, a music ashram!

Remarkably, when I was at the Devi Music Ashram, I also

met Sandro Shankara from Brazil, who was leading a group of spiritual seekers to Rishikesh. We met and immediately became friends; he did want my guitar! He is truly a spiritual shaman, and I am so thankful he was able to participate and to bring along to the audiobook Felipe Mercandelli as Duabu Sam and Sandro's amazing wife Carol Santosha as Irani.

When you write a book, you learn a lot. I was led to research about the Amazon rainforest and then also about indigenous peoples in the Americas. Native Americans are remarkable people, and we can learn so much about life from them. I had not found anyone to read the Native American parts when one day, as I was listening to Native American music in my car, he popped into my mind; Verdell Primeaux. I have several albums from this two-time Grammy award winning singer, I reached out to him, and we became friends. He read the part of Chief Strong Bear. His wife Pearlene Wilson read the part of Clan Mother Whispering Wind, and their daughter Florinda Wilson read the part of Soft Snow. I am forever grateful.

There were several key roles other than the main characters, too. It took me a while to realize that my good friend Joe Hage would be the perfect voice for Alexander Bozos. Joe is a musician, entertainer, and an Island man like me. His friend Azure Lea happened along at just the right time to play Speaker Nancee.

Our representative in Congress is Jamie Raskin, who I have met several times and then realized he played piano. So, I asked him to do a Planetary Gig Talk podcast interview and he agreed. He is an amazing person and smart Constitutional scholar. Unbeknownst to him, I had modeled Congressman Hoyez Jazzkin on Jamie (with a tip of the hat also to Steny

Hoyer). Dave Welsch read this part perfectly. Thank you, Congressman; let's save American democracy!

It's a very fortunate thing when your wife is also Mother Earth! I want to thank my wife Julie Littell for reading the part of Mother Earth and putting up with all this fonging and musical craziness! We've created a wonderful life together, still surviving the pandemic, and looking forward to many more happy years. Love ya, Jules!

I'm not really sure where some of the characters came from; all of a sudden, the trees were talking! I heard the melodious voice of Resa Gibbs as the Trees, and she agreed to read that part. It wasn't a great leap then to ask the multi-talented Jackie Merritt to read the part of the Spirit of Music. I am very thankful these two wonderful musicians and friends could be involved; after all, their pictures are actually in the original *Fonging for the Soul* book!

I also figured that there should be some sort of foreword or intro, but decided I'd rather have the audiobook start right off with the story. So, I thought having comments at the end of the book might be an idea, focusing on looking back at the book, and then forward to the future. I've had the wonderful pleasure of many deep conversations about musical topics with Roy 'Futureman' Wooten, and I knew he would come up with some incisive comments. We ended up with an Onward chapter at the end, and Roy sounded so good when he sent me recordings of him reading the book, it seemed obvious we were also meant to have a second audiobook with Roy reading it. Truth and experimenting! Roy is such a brilliant musician, it's a privilege to have him as an important contributor to this project.

Thanks to my musical brother Dylan Hughes for the Fonging song that leads off the chapters. Also gratitude to Jeff Covert for helping me with the Ho'oponopono song and the cup clapping!

Many thanks also to the friends and family who helped me and consulted along the way, beginning with my brother John Haywood Glassie, who really gave me encouragement and validation, and his daughter Natalie. My cousin Henry Glassie and his wife Pravina Shukla helped too; she assisted me in describing the attire and food from India. Nate Dowery is a friend who reminded me to include Lift Every Voice in the book; so thankful for that and Gaye's rendition of it was awesome.

Patricia Raine is a good friend and musician, and she instigated and enhanced conversations we had for Planetary Gig Talk Live! about music and ho'oponopono and morphic resonance, and really helped me early on with the spiritual connotations of fonging. Peter McClard is an amazing musician and author, and he helped me think outside the box about how to create an invisible island outside of space and time!

My good friend and great musician Allen Holmes was instrumental in new perspectives on Mother Earth and the Spirit of Music, and I am very thankful for his insights and our conversations. Jane Perini and Wib Middleton also talked with me along the way about the book, and then Jane ended up designing the printed version of the book! Thanks also to their daughter Adalia Tara who is a fantastic singer, musician, and inspiration. My friend Alixe Landry who I met at Spirit of Music camp was one of the first people I told about this idea

of the angel coming to the granddaughter to teach her fonging, and I am thankful she didn't think it was a crazy idea!

I'd also like to leave you with a few literary references, in
no particular order; these are books I'd suggest you check out
if you're interested in some of the various rabbit holes this
book goes down:

- *Love is Letting Go of Fear* by Gerald Jampolsky
- *The Amazon, What Everyone Needs to Know* by Mark
  Plotkin
- *Indian Givers* by Jack Weatherford
- *The Music Lesson* and *The Spirit of Music* by Victor Wooten
- *Braiding Sweetgrass* by Robin Wall Kimmerer
- *Societies of Peace; Matriarchies Past, Present and Future*
  Edited by Heidi Goettner-Abendroth
- *Morphic Resonance* by Rupert Sheldrake
- *Caste* and the *Warmth of Other Suns* by Isabel Wilkerson
- *Heaven is Everywhere, Peace and Forgiveness, Fonging for
  the Soul* by Jefferson Glassie
- *The World is Sound – Nada Brahma* by Joachim-Ernst
  Berendt
- *Electric Body, Electric Health* and *Tuning the Human
  Biofield* by Eileen Day McKusick
- *Effortless Mastery* by Kenny Werner
- *Zero Limits* by Joe Vitale and Dr. Hew Len

Thanks of course to all my family, Jay and Chloe, Anne
and Andrew, Mae, Theo, and Rosemary, and Max, my sister
Claire and her family, and all the Littells who shared their
family zooms during the pandemic (the conversations were

lifesaving), and our bubble friend Jennifer Katzka, who also read and heard me talk about this stuff over many zooms and dinners.

Finally, let me give credit to the music in the book. Dylan Hughes wrote and performed the music for the fonging song between chapters. I wrote the "I love my path" affirmation and came up with the music with Kathleen Hooper. I wrote the lyrics for "Money is Like a River," and Dave "Razz" Rasmussen provided the music, which Gaye Adegbalola and Katheen Hooper sang so well. Devi sang the song "Vaishnav Jan to Tene Kahiye Je Peed Parae Jane Je," written by Narsinh Mehta, and Raj played sitar. "Pachamama" is a traditional song of the Amazon, which was sung by Sandro Shankara and his wife Carol Santosha. The lyrics to "Lift Every Voice and Sing" were written by James Weldon Johnson in about 1900 initially as a poem, with the music added a few years later by his brother Rosamond Johnson, and the NAACP dubbed it the Negro National Anthem in 1919. Gaye Adegbalola played and sang the song powerfully with an arrangement Nate Dowery and I had come up with; the song always brings tears to my eyes. Lastly, I took the Ho'oponopono words and added to them, and sang that with Gaye Adegbalola, Queen Lovelace, and Jeff Covert. Many thanks to Music!

Pax Vobiscum,
Jefferson

Jefferson Glassie has been studying and writing about concepts of peace for most of his adult life. It's sort of an obsession. His main goals in life are to have peace of mind and bring peace to the earth. He's still working at it. It's become much easier with music leading the way. He really did write *Fonging for the Soul* under the pseudonym Erasmus Caffery and is the Fongmaster.

He also is the chief spiritual dude of the Planetary Gigs Society and has interviewed many musicians and others about the power of music through the Planetary Gig Talk podcast, and lead many discussions about the various aspects of music as part of the Planetary Gig Talk Live! program. He also has partnered with bluegrass musician Tara Linhardt on the Planetary Music Project video show, where they visit different musicians and musical communities around the world to show the commonalities we all have through music. As another program of the Planetary Gigs Society, Glassie has organized many Concerts for Democracy, virtual and in person, and hopes to continue those to support our freedoms. He founded the International Music Ashram Association to promote establishment of music ashrams around the world to support music and musicians.

He is almost retired from his profession as a lawyer for nonprofit membership associations. He lives in Bethesda, Maryland with his wife Julie Littell aka Mother Earth and treasures his children Jay, Anne, and Max, and his grandchildren Mae, Theo, and Rosemary, and his entire family and all humans. His retirement plan is music.